M5

S0-CAN-301

"Maybe you should really consider getting a wife?" Shelby suggested hesitantly.

"Totally out of the question. Absolutely and positively no!"

Shelby blinked.

Patrick continued, "Maybe you can guess—my first venture into marriage wasn't the greatest thing since sliced bread."

For a moment Shelby didn't register what he'd said. She'd just had the most incredible idea.

"Maybe not a real wife," she said slowly, thinking aloud. "But what about a paper one? Someone, say, who worked where there was child care provided for employees. Who would be glad to help you out in your time of need, in exchange for services in her time of need."

Patrick's eyes narrowed. "Don't tell me, let me guess. The paragon happens to be you."

Dear Reader,

Welcome to BEAUFORT BRIDES, a trilogy about three
sisters who untangle a web of deceit from the past and
discover that the solving of this puzzle leads to a gorgeous
bridegroom and a glorious wedding for each of them!

My three heroines, Margot, Shelby and Georgia, are all
very different, yet their qualities complement each other
perfectly. Margot has a strong sense of responsibility,
Shelby is quiet and shy and Georgia is outrageous and
daring. I like to think that I have something of each of
these women in myself!

I had a wonderful time developing stories for these
remarkable sisters and the extraspecial men in their lives.
Together, they determine to follow their hearts until the
truth about their father is revealed. I invite you to come
and see....

Barbara McMahon

Look out for Georgia's story in
Georgia's Groom (#3620).
On sale September 2000.

A MOTHER FOR MOLLIE
Barbara McMahon

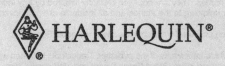

TORONTO • NEW YORK • LONDON
AMSTERDAM • PARIS • SYDNEY • HAMBURG
STOCKHOLM • ATHENS • TOKYO • MILAN • MADRID
PRAGUE • WARSAW • BUDAPEST • AUCKLAND

If you purchased this book without a cover you should be aware
that this book is stolen property. It was reported as "unsold and
destroyed" to the publisher, and neither the author nor the
publisher has received any payment for this "stripped book."

ISBN 0-373-03616-7

A MOTHER FOR MOLLIE

First North American Publication 2000.

Copyright © 2000 by Barbara McMahon.

All rights reserved. Except for use in any review, the reproduction or
utilization of this work in whole or in part in any form by any electronic,
mechanical or other means, now known or hereafter invented, including
xerography, photocopying and recording, or in any information storage
or retrieval system, is forbidden without the written permission of the
publisher, Harlequin Enterprises Limited, 225 Duncan Mill Road,
Don Mills, Ontario, Canada M3B 3K9.

All characters in this book have no existence outside the imagination of
the author and have no relation whatsoever to anyone bearing the same
name or names. They are not even distantly inspired by any individual
known or unknown to the author, and all incidents are pure invention.

This edition published by arrangement with Harlequin Books S.A.

® and TM are trademarks of the publisher. Trademarks indicated with
® are registered in the United States Patent and Trademark Office, the
Canadian Trade Marks Office and in other countries.

Visit us at www.eHarlequin.com

Printed in U.S.A.

CHAPTER ONE

SHELBY Beaufort hesitated at the door. She should have called. But after so many refusals, and fruitless appointments that she hoped would pan out, and hadn't, she wanted a face-to-face confrontation. She knew Patrick O'Shaunnessy was reliable. Didn't the company she worked for use him repeatedly? Of course she had never met the man. Wiping her palms along her skirt, she lifted her chin and took a deep breath.

Opening the door, she stepped into a small waiting area. There was no one behind the desk. Glancing at her watch, she saw it was just shy of five o'clock. She'd left work early to see the man. Had his secretary also left early?

"Hello, is anyone here?" she called.

The door to her right snapped open and a tall man filled the space, fists on his hips, surveying her from head to toe.

"Looking for someone?" he asked.

She nodded, amazed at his height—easily six feet five inches. When her gaze traveled up, she noticed he was topped by hair as black as midnight, with eyes as blue as the Irish sea. His face looked as if it had been hewn from the Irish cliffs themselves, all angles and planes. Not particularly handsome, but arresting.

Intriguing.

Fascinating.

Instantly she wondered how he could make a living

5

as a private investigator. She could not envision Patrick O'Shaunnessy creeping around incognito spying on cheating spouses or eavesdropping on criminal planning. He was too conspicuous. Too fascinating.

Not to mention intimidating.

Maybe a telephone call would have been better. But she was already here, too late for would-have-beens.

"I want to hire you to find someone for me," she blurted out, already regretting she had not made an appointment first. But she didn't want to be refused again.

He lifted a dark eyebrow. Glancing around the office, he frowned. "Where's Joyce?"

"Who?"

"My secretary cum office manager." Scowling, he strode to the desk, snatched up a paper and read it quickly.

"Well, damn. She's quit. She threatened it, but I didn't think she meant it." Running his left hand through his raven hair, he left it messed and falling across his forehead. Shelby tightened her grip on her purse to keep from giving in to the surprising urge to step closer and brush it back into place.

Had she lost her mind? She hadn't come here to indulge in some sort of instant, unexpected attraction to a stranger. She needed a private investigator and he was the last one on her list. She'd shied away from contacting him at first—because of his association with the insurance company she worked for. But after being refused by a half-dozen agencies in New Orleans, she had run out of names. Private investigators were supposed to be discreet. If he took her case, she'd rely on his keeping quiet as to the nature of her request. And it would not involve any kind of conflict of interest connected with her company.

"There was no one here when I came in," she offered.

"I had a secretary. She stormed out a couple of hours ago. She just wrote a note and quit." He looked hopefully over to the other door which stood partially ajar. There was no one in that office, though following his glance, Shelby saw it was larger than the reception area, with two desks and a bank of phones and computer equipment.

"Guess they're both out," he said.

"Who?"

"The two operatives who work for me."

"Oh." She tried to follow the conversation, but it wasn't getting to the point of her visit.

"Mr. O'Shaunnessy," she began. "I wish to retain your services to locate a missing person."

She'd been through the drill now six times. She knew it by rote.

He looked at her. "File a report with the cops?"

She shook her head.

"Why not? If a person is missing, they'll find him or her for free."

"Well, I'm not sure he's precisely missing—I just don't know where he is."

He glanced at his watch. "I'd love to hear about a missing person who isn't missing, but I have to pick up my daughter at day care and need to leave now. If I'm not there by six, she's history with them."

"I beg your pardon?"

"You don't want to know, lady. Come back in the

morning—but not before nine. There'll be someone here then." He headed back into his office.

Dumbfounded, Shelby remained where she stood. He wasn't even taking the time to listen to her. At least someone at each of the other agencies had listened. One investigator had even agreed to help her. The proposed estimated expense had proved too prohibitive, however. Would she find that the case here as well?

Patrick reappeared in only seconds, shrugging into a sports coat.

"Since neither of my operatives are here, I need to lock up," he said, opening the outside door and clearly waiting for her to leave.

"But I want to hire you," Shelby protested. It had taken a lot of planning to get here before five; she didn't intend to be dismissed so easily. Normally quiet and shy, she was growing more and more frustrated with how difficult it was to hire an investigator and that made her more determined than ever!

"Not today. I need to get to the preschool."

"Where is it? I'll ride along," she said recklessly. She could not take time off from work in the morning to talk to him. She'd already taken a lot of time off to do her part in settling her grandmother's estate. Her boss had been very understanding, but there was a limit.

Patrick looked at her in surprise. "I don't do business in my car."

Planting herself directly in front of him, Shelby stared up into his face. She had to get him to change his mind.

Patrick looked at her, noticing how tall she was. She had to be five foot nine or ten. Most women made him feel like Gulliver in Lilliput Land. Not this one. She came to his chin and for one crazy moment he realized how easy it would be to kiss her—no contortions like he normally needed with the shorter women he usually dated.

When he dated, which hadn't been often in the last year.

Of course, if he'd met someone like this before, he might have been inclined to make more of an effort.

He shook his head. He didn't have time for such idle speculation—he had a deadline to meet! Any interest in a new case came second to his little girl.

"What's your name?" he asked.

"Shelby Beaufort."

"Well, Shelby Beaufort, I have a kid to pick up. I can't be late. Not again. If you would call in the morning—"

"Maybe I should just try elsewhere," she said sharply.

Patrick held back an epithet. He needed the money a new case would bring in. Things hadn't gone smoothly over the last year because of the changes in his life with the arrival on his doorstep of his daughter Mollie. He couldn't afford to turn away work.

But neither could he afford to be late again.

"Come on, then, Shelby Beaufort. Ever consider a career in private investigation? You're stubborn enough to qualify."

Shelby shook her head as she followed him down the hall and struggled to keep up with his long, impatient stride. Patrick wasn't going to slow down. She could keep up or come another time.

At least he was going to hear her out, Shelby thought

gratefully as she attempted to keep pace with the man. He seemed to be heading for the multilevel parking structure around the block from his building. The late June afternoon was sultry and hot. Surreptitiously she pulled her blouse away from her damp skin. Glaring at him she noticed he didn't appear to be affected by the high temperature at all.

She, on the other hand, felt wrung out and about to melt in a heap.

When he stopped beside a beat-up old vehicle, she looked at it in surprise.

"This is your car?" Maybe he wasn't doing as well as she thought. Was he truly the investigator she wanted?

He smiled sardonically and opened his door. "Climb in, it's not locked. Who'd want to steal this wreck?"

Almost nodding in agreement, Shelby opened the passenger door, wincing at the loud screech it emitted. Gingerly she slid onto the seat. Surprisingly the inside of the car was immaculate. Ignoring the screech, she pulled the door shut with a strong thump.

He started the car, the engine turning over instantly, almost purring. Cool air was soon blasting from the vents.

"Sounds all right, anyway," she murmured, buckling her seat belt.

"Camouflage," he muttered. "Some of the places I go I don't want people to notice me. Who pays attention to a beat- up old car? But she has a top-notch engine."

She held on for dear life as he roared out to the parking garage as if to prove the prowess of the engine. Minutes later they were embroiled in New Orleans' rush hour traffic. They crawled along Magnolia Street, inching through four traffic signals before turning onto Canal Street.

Patrick wasn't the most patient of men. He beat a rough tattoo on the steering wheel, muttering under his breath and checking his watch at least once a minute.

Shelby wondered when he would bring up her request. He seemed to have forgotten her. She cleared her throat.

"About my hiring you," she said.

Patrick looked at her. "Okay, babe, let's hear the scoop."

Shelby winced. No one had ever called her *babe* before. She looked out of the front window as Patrick just missed crashing into the back of the car in front of them. She winced again.

"I want you to locate my father," she said, afraid to take her eyes off the traffic. Maybe she could warn him next time. Or at least brace herself for the impact.

"Name?"

"Sam Williams."

"Age?"

"I don't know exactly." She needed to explain to the man she didn't remember her father, that he'd left when she'd been just a toddler.

"Have a birth certificate?"

"For him?"

"No, for you."

"I can get one, I guess."

"It'll be on that. Unless your mother didn't name him as the father."

Shelby drew herself up, turning outraged eyes on the man.

"My parents were married. Of course my mother would have listed him as the father. They were very much in love."

Patrick snorted, and leaned on the horn as a motorcyclist tried to cut in. The man shot a look at Patrick and accelerated between two other cars, weaving his way through traffic.

"I should get one of those," Patrick muttered.

"Mr. O'Shaunnessy."

"Call me Patrick, and I'll call you Shelby. So how long has your father been missing? And why don't you know how old he is?"

"He left Natchez when I was two. That's twenty-three years ago."

He turned and looked at her. "Any reason for the delay in reporting this? I mean twenty-three years is a lot of time to sit on a missing person report. Didn't you notice he was missing during that time?"

"Actually, I'm not sure he considers himself missing. There were extenuating circumstances regarding his leaving. In fact, until just a few months ago, we thought he'd left voluntarily. Then we discovered he hadn't."

She twisted the straps of her purse and cringed when he pulled around a slow car, accelerated strongly then slammed on the brakes. They'd gained about fifty feet. Now traffic ahead of them was at a standstill.

"Blast it." Patrick pounded the stirring wheel again.

"Is there a problem?" Shelby asked, wondering if she'd made a tactical mistake in insisting she go with him. His driving skills were frightening. Maybe *skills* was too strong a word. She hoped she survived the experience long enough to reap any of the benefit hiring a private investigator might provide.

"I can't believe the traffic!"

"It's always bad at this time of day. I used to drive to work, but switched to walking and public transportation. It was easier." And a lot less stressful, but she didn't think she should mention that at this particular moment.

When he looked at his watch again and frowned, she had to ask, "Are we under some kind of time deadline?"

"You got it in one, sister. If I don't get my kid out of the day care by six, she's history."

"You mentioned that before. I can't believe the facility would be so inflexible as to enforce such a ruling. Surely parents are a few minutes late from time to time."

He shot her a glance and grinned. "Probably. And they were good about it the first dozen times. But it's chronic with us."

She cleared her throat. "Can't your wife pick up your child?"

"Nope, been dead for more than a year."

She opened her mouth to ask another question, but he raised his hand. "And before you start on another line of inquiry, I'll tell you so far I haven't been able to keep a housekeeper any longer than I can keep a secretary."

Shelby darted him a dark glance. Somehow she wasn't surprised to hear that. He about drove her crazy and she'd only met him about an hour ago.

"About my father," she said, changing the subject.

"Can't do it. Try the police."

Disappointed, she considered her other options. At least he wasn't trying to charge enough money to pay off the national debt. But darn it, he wasn't taking her seriously.

"I don't think the police will help. I just want someone to locate him."

"And do what?"

She blinked. She hadn't even thought that far ahead, she acknowledged. "Just locate him and tell me where he is."

"After twenty-three years? That might not be so easy. What have you got for me to go on?"

"His name, and if I get his age from my birth certificate, I can give you that. I do know he worked as an oil wildcatter twenty-three years ago. The company he worked for might have a forwarding address or something."

"Did you try asking them?"

She shook her head. "I don't know which company he worked for."

"Great."

He pulled off the jammed street onto a quiet one, winding his way through the modest neighborhood. He slammed to a stop by a colorful school. A little girl dressed in denim overalls, white shirt, with a small baseball cap on her brown hair sat forlornly on the front steps. In her arms were papers and paintings and one ragged teddy bear. Beside her stood an older woman.

Shelby knew by the tight-lipped expression on the woman's face that Patrick had missed his deadline.

He checked his watch.

"Ten minutes late! You'd think they'd give me ten lousy minutes."

He thrust open the car door and strode over to the little girl.

Shelby watched as the child popped up from her step and raced to her father. Rolling down the window, letting out the lingering air-conditioned coolness and feeling the rush of sticky humid air, Shelby strained to hear what she was saying.

"I haff to take all my stuff," she said, offering her father the stack of papers, but retaining hold on the teddy bear.

The older woman walked down the sidewalk. "Mr. O'Shaunnessy. I'm sorry, but the center just can't allow this. We have been more then lenient with you. More so than any other parent in our group. But it is unfair to continue to expect us to bend the rules for you. I'm afraid you'll have to find other arrangements for Mollie."

She handed him a large manila envelope.

"This contains her records. Good luck." She gave Mollie a quick hug and said something to the little girl. Shelby was relieved to find the woman could smile. At least she didn't leave the little girl thinking she was mad at her.

When she looked at Patrick, however, her heart skipped a beat. For such a large man, he looked curiously vulnerable. He squatted down near the little girl. Even so he still seemed huge. Reaching out an arm, he scooped her up and began walking slowly back to the car.

When Mollie caught sight of Shelby, she ducked her head close to her father.

"Who's that?" she asked, studying Shelby warily.

"That's Shelby."

"Is she my new baby-sitter?"

"No, she's—" Patrick looked at her and shrugged. "She's just Shelby."

He made sure the little girl was buckled in the back-seat and climbed behind the wheel.

Leaning back against the seat, he stared out the window.

"Let's go, Daddy, I'm hungry," Mollie said.

"We have to drop Shelby back at the office so she can get her car," he said.

"I can find my own way back," she said. It would probably be safer than a return trip with Patrick's wild driving. He'd made his position clear on her request, so there was really no need to continue this farce of a meeting. Tomorrow she'd have to go through the phone book again and see what other agencies she could try. She was not giving up!

"No, we'll take you back. My mama taught me to take a woman all the way home. In this case, all the way to your car will suffice." He started the engine.

Patrick hated having to fight his way through the traffic again to return to the office. But he still had to get to that side of town to go home. Maybe while there, he could find something for Mollie to snack on. If he picked up some files to take home, he'd be that much farther ahead in the morning. With no baby-sitter and no day care for tomorrow, he'd be stuck at home with Mollie while he looked for someone to take care of her.

"There are other day care facilities," Shelby said softly.

"I know, we've been in most of them." He wondered if the first one would give them another chance. It had been almost a year.

"What you need is a housekeeper who would be able to watch your daughter at home. Then you wouldn't have to worry about quitting time or meeting deadlines."

He looked at her. "What insight!" He shook his head, "Don't you think I've tried that route? What I need, Miss-Shelby-Beaufort-with-a-father-missing-for-twenty-three years is a *wife*. Someone who would be there for Mollie all the time, not just during the day. Someone who could cook decent meals so we don't eat out so much at fast food places, and someone to keep clothes washed, hair trimmed. And someone who couldn't quit at the first sign of trouble." He glanced in the mirror, angled to see his daughter. She was talking to her teddy and seemed oblivious to the conversation in the front seat.

"Maybe you should consider that, then," Shelby said.

"Nope, tried that once—it didn't work."

It seemed unfair that the traffic on the return was much lighter. Patrick drove calmly. Shelby wasn't scared once. She was even a bit reluctant to say good-bye when he stopped near her car.

She shut the screeching door, and looked over the roof of the car when Patrick stood on his side.

"You'll be all right?" he asked.

"I may call again about your locating my father."

"First I need to locate someone to watch Mollie. There's a lot you can do on your own. Try your birth certificate first. Then the company where he used to work if you can find out which one it was, or call around to the ones still in business. No sense wasting your money if you can discover the answer on your own.''

''Thanks for the suggestions.'' She hesitated, but there was really nothing else. ''Goodbye,'' Shelby said, wishing she didn't have to leave. There was something about the man that continued to intrigue her.

Patrick's words echoed that evening while Shelby prepared a light supper. Frustrated not to have an acceptance for her assignment, she paced her small kitchen while she waited for the gumbo to heat. She was finding it much more difficult to hire a private investigator than she expected.

Either they weren't interested, like Patrick, or they wanted half of Fort Knox as an up-front retainer—with no guarantee they could come up with anything.

It had been four months since her older sister, Margot, had discovered that their father had not abandoned them as children as they had been told all their lives by their grandmother, Harriet Beaufort. He had, instead, been forced away from his wife and family by Harriet's machinations. She'd wanted a different alliance for her only daughter and had done her best to bring that about.

Shelby wondered what would have happened if her mother had not died so soon after her father had been threatened with a bogus murder charge and driven from the family home in Natchez. Would her mother have found the strength and courage to search for her husband, or would she have given in to the demands of her strong-willed mother and turned to the man whose family fortune and historical lineage had been so important to Harriet Beaufort?

It didn't matter. Her mother had died shortly after Shelby's younger sister's birth—leaving her three daughters to be raised by Harriet.

Now her grandmother was dead and in dying had revealed the shameful situation to Shelby's sister Margot. When her sister had discovered proof of her grandmother's interference, it had satisfied a need in her to know for certain that their father had not abandoned them.

Of course, Margot's reconciliation with her husband and discovering she was pregnant had taken her mind off searching for their father. Now living in the Garden District of New Orleans, renovating and restoring a huge old house she and Rand had bought recently, and trying to open a new branch of her own interior design business, Margot's life was totally full.

And happy.

Shelby didn't resent her sister's delight in her husband and the longed-for baby, but she was a bit envious.

And her younger sister Georgia had her new job. She had branched into trauma nursing, taking additional courses, working in the emergency room of one of New Orleans' busiest hospitals. She rarely spoke of the father who had left before she was born. And Shelby didn't bring him up often. But she ached to know what had happened to the man she didn't remember, but had missed all her life.

Giving the gumbo a stir, she vowed she wasn't going to stop now. She'd try Patrick's suggestions and see where they led. And if needed, she'd approach him again. If he refused to help, she'd go back to the phone book and check out another agency. And another— until she found someone willing to take on the assignment. Even if her father was dead, she wanted to know where Sam Williams had lived and what he'd done with his life.

Friday morning Patrick poured another cup of coffee and swallowed a mouthful. It burned all the way down. He didn't notice. He'd been on the phone for hours over the last two days, trying to find a day care with an opening for Mollie.

It looked as if he'd run out of options.

His operatives had called a dozen times. One client had called, tracking him down at home, because of an error in the billing. And of course he had no secretary to look into it. Joyce had probably invoiced the wrong amount, but he would have to go to the office to get it straightened out.

And what would he do with Mollie?

The doorbell rang.

"I'll get it!" Mollie's voice called out as he heard her racing for the door.

"No!" he yelled. She loved to open the door, but caution made sure he always knew who was there before letting her. Most of his cases were innocuous, paper tracing, but one never knew these days when some nut would seek him out for an imagined slight.

He looked through the peephole and then leaned his head against the door.

He didn't need this.

Opening it, he stared at Shelby Beaufort. Standing

squarely in the center of the doorway, he wanted to block any attempt at entry.

"Hello, Patrick," Shelby said brightly. "I've come to discuss the case."

"There is no case. I thought I told you a few days ago I couldn't help you."

"Please, I've taken time from work I can ill afford." She grinned and shrugged. "I told them I was sick. I got the information you told me I could find. I forgot to tell you that we found someone not too long ago who actually knew our father. You can ask her questions we didn't think of."

"You can handle that yourself." He held Mollie back when she tried to insert herself between him and the doorjamb.

"At least listen to what I've got, please. Finding my father is really important to me."

"Yeah, well, so's keeping my kid important to me, and I don't think either one is going to happen." He turned and swept Mollie up in his arm and made to shut the door.

"Wait." Shelby stepped inside, crowding against Patrick and Mollie. Her behavior was diametrically opposed to what she was used to doing, but she was getting desperate.

Patrick glared at her and then softened his expression as he looked at his daughter. "Why don't you get your bear and head back for your room? As soon as Shelby leaves, we'll have lunch."

"Okay." The little girl ducked her head and looked at Shelby with wide, curious eyes.

"She wears a baseball hat even in the house?" Shelby asked.

"Yes, do you have a problem with that?" His tone was belligerent.

Shelby smiled at Mollie and shook her head.

When the little girl ran off down the hall, Patrick leaned against the hall wall and crossed his arms over his chest.

"I don't know how to make myself any clearer. I don't want to find your father. I've got other things of greater concern right now."

"What do you mean by your comment about keeping your daughter? Didn't you find a new day care center?"

He looked across the street, catching sight of his neighbor avidly staring in his direction. Her curiosity knew no bounds.

"You might as well come inside, no sense the whole world hearing." And it would give him some small satisfaction to shut the door on Mrs. Turner's snooping.

Shelby looked around and saw Patrick's neighbor. She smiled politely and stepped aside so he could shut the door.

Glancing around, she noted a child's clutter—books, crayons, toys, blocks. The TV sounded from the front room. Had she interrupted cartoons?

"This way," he said leading the way down the hall into the small kitchen. A table shoved against the wall held the remnants of their breakfast. Shelby said nothing, sitting gingerly on the chair he indicated.

"How did you find me?" he asked, sitting in another chair and tilting back on its rear legs.

"One of the operatives at your office said you were working from home and sent me here when I said you were handling a case for me."

"Thought we cleared up the situation a couple of days ago," he said. "I'm not handling anything until I get Mollie situated."

"I've contacted three more agencies—from listings in the phone book. They all said no, but one of them recommended you. Not that I needed the recommendation. You occasionally do some work for Acme Insurance Company—my employers. I figure that's about the best recommendation I can get. A search like this can't be that hard for someone as experienced as you. But I don't have a clue where to begin. I didn't even think of the birth certificate angle to obtain my father's age."

"Lady, I have a lot of other things on my mind right now. The last thing I need is to take on a new case."

"Business is so good you can refuse it?" she asked in surprise.

He slammed down the front legs of his chair, rose and crossed to the stove. "Want some coffee?"

"That would be nice."

"Business is going to hell in a handbasket, but I can't concentrate on that without getting Mollie settled first." He filled two cups and brought them to the table. Placing one before Shelby, he took a sip of his and began to pace.

"If I don't find something soon, my goose is cooked."

Shelby licked her lips. "A live-in baby-sitter?"

"Tried that—had four. One quit right in the middle of the day."

At her look of surprise, he shrugged. "Mollie's a bit spoiled. She can throw a terrific tantrum if it suits her."

"And day care is out?"

He nodded toward the phone. "I've been calling for two days straight. Either they're full, or they charge half a year's income, or they're ones we've already been thrown out of."

Shelby looked at him, trying to swallow the urge to giggle at the image. From what she'd seen of Mollie, the little girl was delightful. Must be his propensity for tardiness.

"It's not funny. If I don't find something soon, I may have to let Mollie go to her grandmother's."

"So there is someone to watch her."

"Yeah, she just happens to live in Atlanta."

"Oh."

"It's the last thing I want to do."

Shelby nodded in agreement. "Little girls need their fathers. I know. I didn't have one."

He glared at her. "If there was another way, don't you think I'd leap at it? Fathers happen to want their little girls, too."

Stunned, Shelby tried to figure out if her father had hated leaving. If he had missed his daughters all these years as much as she'd missed him. Wouldn't he have done all he could to see them? she wondered. She could sympathize with Patrick O'Shaunnessy's desire to keep his daughter.

"Maybe you should really consider getting a wife," she suggested hesitantly.

"Totally out of the question. Absolutely and positively *no!* Good God, I think I'd kill myself first."

Shelby blinked. "So why don't you tell me how you really feel about the suggestion, Patrick?"

CHAPTER TWO

HE stopped pacing and leaned against the wall, sipping from his cup.

"Maybe you can guess, my first venture into marriage wasn't the greatest thing since sliced bread."

For a moment Shelby didn't register what he'd said. She'd just had the most incredible idea. It was the most outlandish scheme she'd ever thought of. And Georgia was usually the one in the family to come up with outrageous ideas. Still, it was a measure of how desperately she wanted to locate her father, and how frustrated she felt with no progress in the time she'd been trying.

"Maybe not a real wife," she said slowly, thinking aloud. "What about a paper one?"

Turning so she could face him, she warmed to her idea.

"Someone, say, who worked where there was childcare provided for employees. Who would be glad to help you out in your time of need in exchange for your services in her time of need."

His eyes narrowed. "Don't tell me, let me guess. The paragon just happens to be you."

She nodded. "Think about it for a minute. You have something I need—expertise in tracing lost persons. I have something you can't seem to get—day care for your daughter."

25

"So you take her into that child-care at your work? Where does the marriage bit come in?"

"That's the sticky part—only children, or legal stepchildren, of employees can use the day care center. But there's no question of it being crowded, or even costing anything. And it would eliminate any worry of anyone kicking Mollie out if I'm a few minutes late picking her up. It's set up to accommodate occasional late work by parents. What do you think?"

"I think you're nuts. Absolutely certifiable."

But he narrowed his eyes and gazed at her closely. Shelby could almost see the wheels turning in his mind.

She regarded him gravely. "Maybe. I'm not sure I can explain it. All my life I've been curious about the man who helped create me. Until a little while ago, my sisters and I thought he'd abandoned us when we were babies. But we recently found out differently."

"Sounds like abandonment to me—if he never got in touch with you in twenty-some years. What makes you think he wants to be found? Or wants to establish any kind of contact?"

"Oh, I don't want to contact him necessarily. Just find out what happened to him. See if he needs anything. I make a good salary at the insurance company. Margot has a huge house now in the Garden District, with extra bedrooms and all. Between us, we could do something for him if he needs help."

"He could be dead."

She nodded.

"I almost wish that were so. It would make it easier to know he couldn't have returned than to know he just turned his back on us and kept going," she said slowly.

"But it doesn't matter, I want to know what happened to him. I really need to know, or go crazy."

"So for the price of finding out, you're willing to marry a stranger?"

She hesitated a moment, then nodded.

"Temporarily. And a marriage of convenience would suit both of us, don't you think?" Her heart raced. She'd never proposed anything so crazy before in her life. Yet the thought of that precious, spoiled little girl going hundreds of miles away from her father really hit Shelby hard. She would have given anything to have had her father be part of her life when she was growing up. For a moment she could see herself as that young girl who had so desperately wanted a daddy. The thought of Mollie losing hers was too much.

"What I think is that you are crazy."

Shelby rose and crossed to the sink. "Actually, maybe you're right. I can see all the advantages on your side, and little on mine. Would you expect me to wash all these dishes?" The sink was piled high.

He stepped beside her and tugged her away. "I don't need another wife."

She smiled up at him. "Yes, you do. I could cook dinner, make sure Mollie went to bed on time every night. And free you from all domestic worries so you could find my father. The perfect business arrangement!"

He nodded. "If that's all it is?"

She scanned him from head to toe, then met his gaze. "Afraid I want you for some other nefarious purpose?"

He laughed at that and shook his head. Walking to his chair he dropped down on it, putting his empty cup on the table. "Not with a face like mine. How long do you propose we stay married?"

"I don't know, until we no longer have to be, I guess." She hadn't thought that far ahead. In fact, if she did any thinking at all, she'd probably realize this was one of the dumbest ideas she'd ever come up with. Marriage wasn't something to tumble into and then out of.

Yet, if it enabled her to locate her father, it would be worth it. And she liked children. She and Mollie would probably get along great. And she would help keep a little girl with her daddy.

"So you'd be Mollie's stepmama for a while?"

"I wouldn't do anything to worm my way into her affections. I wouldn't want her to miss me when we get the marriage annulled. But for the time being she could go to the day care at the company." And Patrick could search for her father.

"Annulled." He held her eyes. "That's what you're planning?"

Flustered, Shelby nodded. Heat rose in her as a totally different image sprang to mind. That of Patrick kissing her, holding her. She shook her head to clear the vision. Whoa, she was looking for a way to enable him to take her case, nothing else!

"I'm proposing a marriage of convenience, not the real thing," she said firmly, wondering if that would end up being enough.

"And in exchange I locate your father."

She nodded again.

"Let me think about it."

"There's one more thing," she said slowly, suddenly feeling awkward. Why now after already broaching the subject she didn't know. But it grew steadily more difficult. Clearing her throat, she tilted her chin. "I'd have to live here for the time being. And we'd have to pretend to my family that it's a real marriage."

"Why?"

"My sister Margot is pregnant. She miscarried during her first pregnancy and we don't want anything upsetting her this time. If we pretend to be married for real, she won't have anything to worry about. We don't have to tell her about our deal. Time enough after the baby is born."

"Let me get this straight—in exchange for searching for your father, we get married, pretend to the world we're madly in love, and you'll take Mollie to day care, live here and cook?"

Shelby nodded slowly. Saying it aloud did make it sound preposterous. Glancing around the kitchen, she smiled brightly. "I'm a great cook."

"Do you realize most of the time I'm in the office during the day and home every night like any businessman, but there are occasions when I need to go somewhere on business or handle a surveillance, or monitor some particular activity which means I won't be home that night? Are you willing to watch Mollie under those circumstances?"

"Of course. I'll be living here." She didn't want to tell him she normally didn't have much to do in the evenings. That would lead to all sorts of questions she didn't care to answer.

He studied her for a long moment, then rose.

"I'll think about your offer."

Feeling let down, Shelby nodded. She was sure once she had a chance to think about what she'd just suggested, she'd change her mind. But for a few minutes it seemed so perfect.

How long could it take him to find her father? Even a few months pretending to be married wouldn't be a hardship. Just until Margot had her baby. She would help him out with Mollie, make sure the little girl stayed with her father and wasn't sent away to Atlanta to live with grandparents.

"I'll leave you my number," she said.

"That won't be necessary. If I can't find you here in New Orleans how do you ever expect me to find your father?" he drawled.

Shelby felt like an idiot as she headed out to the Garden District to visit her sister. Since she wasn't working today, she might as well make the most of her day off. But she continued to think of her meeting with Patrick. What had possessed her to offer a marriage of convenience? The man probably suspected she had ulterior motives and wanted something else.

And she didn't want to involve her sisters. Rand and Margot had enough with their baby coming and renovating their new house. From something Margot had said, Shelby wasn't sure her older sister felt strongly about actually finding their father. She seemed satisfied to learn that he had not abandoned them as children.

Margot had held the belief for years that she'd been the reason for his desertion. Discovering the truth had ended that lie, and gone a long way into making Margot more trusting around men—and her husband Rand in particular.

Shelby and Georgia had discussed trying to find their father, but for the time being, her younger sister was too wrapped up in her new nursing course and her normal duties to have time to explore further.

That left it up to Shelby.

She still remembered how odd she'd felt as a child with no parents. When other girls had their fathers to pick them up from school, or attend the school pageants, or coach soccer, Shelby had no one.

To this day she was uncomfortable around men, never knowing exactly what to talk about, how to treat them. She rarely dated, and then only men she knew from work.

Wistfully she wondered if her father had missed her after he'd left. Whatever he'd done since then didn't matter to her. She just wanted to *know*.

Margot wasn't home. Shelby was disappointed. With nothing else pressing, she headed for the nearest mall. She'd indulge herself by shopping this afternoon. And hope there was a message from Patrick on her answering machine when she returned home.

The phone was ringing when Shelby entered her apartment several hours later and she ran to pick up before it stopped. Had Patrick decided?

"Hi Sis, how are you?" Margot's serene voice came across the line.

"Hi, I'm doing fine. More importantly, how are you?" Shelby ignored the tinge of disappointment she felt that it wasn't Patrick. "Let me call you right back. I just got in and have groceries and things to put away."

"No rush, I just called to chat. Rand's working late tonight. Have your dinner and then call me."

"I'll call you while I eat, dinner won't seem so lonely that way," Shelby said.

While a good cook, she rarely prepared a full meal for herself—saving that effort for when she had friends over. Tonight she heated some soup, toasted French bread and cut up fresh fruit for a salad. Then she called her sister.

She didn't know what Patrick would decide, but just in case, she had better lay the groundwork with her family. Margot would worry just as much with an unexpected wedding as she would knowing the circumstances behind this one.

"I haven't seen you in ages," Margot said, once the preliminaries were out of the way.

"I've been busy," Shelby said, taking a deep breath. "Actually, there's this guy—"

Silence greeted her announcement. She frowned. Was it so shocking that she could attract a man?

"Really?" Margot asked, a hint of excitement in her voice.

"Really. His name is Patrick."

"Where did you meet him? When? Does he work at where you do? How serious are you?" Margot asked.

Shelby laughed at the barrage of questions. "Whoa, slow down. Let's see. I met him at the office." No need to mention which office. "He works for the company sometimes. He's a private investigator." She held her breath. Would Margot suspect?

"Tell all," her sister demanded.

"Well, we've been out a few times." All right, once, to the day care center to pick up Mollie. Not exactly a date, but Margot never needed to know that. And would coffee at his house count?

"It just sort of took off from there."

"What did?"

"Our feelings for each other," Shelby said recklessly.

"My God, you're seriously interested in the man?"

"Definitely!" Seriously interested in having him find their father!

"I can't believe it! Tell me everything. Does Georgia know?"

"Uh, not yet. She's been busy, you've been busy and I've certainly been busy." Looking for a private investigator.

"When can I meet him?"

"There's nothing definite between us yet. I'm not exactly sure how he feels." Except about marriage, she thought with a touch of amusement. He'd made himself perfectly clear on that subject.

"Tell me all about him."

In describing Patrick, Shelby realized she apparently noticed a lot more about the man than she'd thought. Not only his physical characteristics, but some of his mannerisms, like that impatient energy that had to find an outlet in pounding a steering wheel or pacing a small kitchen.

She made no mention of Mollie. If it didn't work out, if she had to find another way to locate her father, she didn't want Margot or Georgia to know more than the bare bones.

"Bring Patrick to dinner on Sunday," Margot ordered.

"I'll have to check and let you know." Shelby panicked. She hadn't expected that. What if Patrick said no to her crazy proposal? What if he refused to go along with a charade to fool her sisters?

"I've got to go now, Margot. Give my love to Rand."

She hung up feeling wrung out. Setting the stage had been difficult. If Patrick agreed to her scheme, could she carry off the deception?

It depended on how badly she wanted to find her father—and protect her sister. Margot had been protecting her all her life. She owed it to her to make sure she kept her from worrying.

The doctor had assured Margot she'd be fine this pregnancy, but Shelby remembered how devastated her older sister had been after her miscarriage and had no intention of being a cause of unnecessary worry or concern.

She was already in bed and leafing through a magazine when the phone rang again.

Her heart skipped a beat when she recognized Patrick's deep voice.

Without any preliminaries he went to the heart of the matter.

"You've got yourself a deal, Shelby."

The enormity of what she'd done almost overwhelmed her.

"Thank you," she said primly.

"Want to discuss particulars now or in the morning?" he asked.

"In the morning." She needed some time to assimilate the fact she would soon be marrying a stranger, pretending an emotion she didn't feel, and be half responsible for a little girl who by her daddy's own admission was spoiled and sometimes threw tantrums.

"We'll pick you up at nine and head for Dunking Delights. Mollie loves donuts."

"Fine."

Hanging up, Shelby stared blankly at the opposite wall. Could she go through with this after all? Or had she just made the biggest mistake of her life?

She shook off her doubts. How hard could it be to pretend for a few hours here and there in front of her sisters that she was a happily married woman? The rest of the time she and Patrick would go their separate ways.

Saturday morning she dressed in yellow shorts and a white loose cotton top. The weather forecaster predicted high temperatures and higher humidity. She wished she lived near the water where there was a chance of a breeze. Instead her apartment was hemmed in by others, keeping any wafts of cool air to a minimum.

Ready long before the appointed time, Shelby paced in front of her window, stopping suddenly when she realized she was copying Patrick.

There was nothing to be nervous about—it was a straightforward business deal. They each brought something that the other needed. And in no time, they'd be able to obtain an annulment and go their separate ways.

But the churning in her stomach didn't abate. Nervously she wiped damp palms on the shorts and began pacing again.

The doorbell startled her. It rang and rang.

Opening the door, she saw Mollie still pressing the button.

"That's enough, Mollie," Patrick said reaching for her hand, his eyes on Shelby.

"I like it," the little girl said, dancing away from her father's reach and spying a doorbell by a nearby door. She raced down the hall and began pressing it.

"Mollie! No!" Patrick called, quickly following after her to snatch her up just as an elderly woman opened her door and peered out.

"Yes?" she said.

"Sorry, Mrs. Hatterly. Mollie's fascinated by doorbells," Shelby said, as she joined Patrick and took his arm, tugging toward her open door. "We didn't mean to bother you."

The older woman nodded vaguely and shut her door.

"It's wrong to ring doorbells if you aren't going to visit the people who live there," Shelby said to Mollie.

"She doesn't know that," Patrick said.

"She'll never learn any younger." Eyeing him suspiciously, she frowned. "Something we might need to discuss, I see."

"What?"

"Discipline."

He took a sharp breath through his nose.

"I'd say we have more than that to discuss. Ready?"

Shelby reached inside for her purse then shut her door. "Ready as I'll ever be." Feeling much like Alice in Wonderland where nothing was quite normal, she headed for the stairs.

Settled at the table for four at the Dunking Delight, Shelby watched Patrick allow Mollie to order two huge jelly-filled donuts. Shelby had eaten her own breakfast a couple of hours ago and settled for a latte.

Once seated, Mollie began to eat, one foot kicking the table leg.

Patrick bit into a light glazed donut.

"Mollie, stop kicking the table, please," Shelby said, patiently.

"Don't gots to," she mumbled, licking jelly from her fingers, her foot swinging again.

"Yes, you do," she said, her tone brooking no refusal.

Patrick looked up at her in surprise.

"She's just a kid," he said defensively.

"Which is the best age to learn proper behavior in public."

Mollie looked from one to the other, her eyes wide. But she stopped kicking the table leg.

"She's four years old," Patrick said.

"And as I mentioned after the doorbells, we obviously need to discuss discipline. Children need rules and boundaries. How do you expect her to learn proper behavior if you don't guide her?"

"She's fine. We don't go out much."

"Oh, that's a great answer. What if you need to go out, do you want a child no one else wants around?"

Mollie's eyes filled with tears.

"Daddy?" she said. "I don't like her."

"I'm beginning to side with you, kid," he said glaring at Shelby. "You're starting to sound like Mollie's grandmother."

Shelby raised an eyebrow. "My sympathies are with the woman."

"Well they shouldn't be. She ruined her daughter and would ruin Mollie if I gave her the chance. Mollie's just a kid. Time enough to learn things later."

"When?" Shelby asked.

"I don't know, later."

She shook her head, took a sip of latte and sighed. It wouldn't work. She had no need to worry about how she'd relate to the father, if she couldn't even relate to the child.

Looking around the restaurant, she noticed other children with their parents. Happy islands in the impersonal public place. A woman laughed at something her son said, while her husband beamed indulgently.

A twinge of envy struck. Shelby would love to be part of a happy family like that. To have a husband who loved her and their children. Who would find time to spend with his family on inconsequential outings like this. A family to build memories with and to reassure their children they were loved.

"Mollie, go play in the kiddy section," Patrick said.

"I'm not done." She'd eaten most of one donut, Shelby noticed when she looked at her. Or at least decimated the donut. It was a toss-up how much was inside and how much smeared on her hands and face. Patrick calmly wiped up as much of the jelly as he could, and sent her to the kiddy area blocked off in one corner of the yard of the restaurant.

Tossing the sticky napkins on the table he narrowed his gaze at her.

"Tell me what makes you such an expert on rearing kids. If my information is correct, you have never married, never had children, never even been exposed to children."

"What information?" she asked, diverted.

He looked guilty for half a second. "A cursory investigation."

"You had me investigated?" Dumbfounded, she could only stare at him.

"I didn't have you investigated, I did it myself. You're twenty-five years old, have an older sister named Margot who is married to Rand Marstall. High circles here in New Orleans. A younger sister named Georgia whom you and everyone else often call Georgie. She's a nurse at St. Joseph's. You were valedictorian at your high school but for some reason elected not to proceed to college but instead got a job at Acme Insurance company where you've worked your way up to a position of lots of responsibility and a certain amount of power and prestige in the company."

"Is that all?" she asked outraged he'd do such a thing. Yet also intrigued he'd found out so much in only a day.

"No current boyfriend," he said slowly. "Of course it was only a quick and dirty look-see, but I don't find information about any boyfriends."

Heat flushed through her cheeks. Except for one boy in high school, he wouldn't find any.

"Maybe I ought to hire an investigator to look into your background," she snapped.

"You're changing the subject. I'm asking about your experience with children."

"Discipline is the word you're looking for, Patrick O'Shaunnessy. And it appears to be sadly lacking in Mollie's life."

"You were raised by your grandmother—some starched-up society dame in Natchez. You probably went to deportment class," he returned.

Shelby almost nodded, but it was none of his business. She was not advocating Mollie be raised as strictly as she and her sisters had been. But there was a happy medium between her deportment lessons and Mollie's free-for-all.

"At least I know how to behave in public," she said as he kept his eyes steadily on her.

"What?"

"Come on, Patrick. Just use common sense. Haven't you been in restaurants where an obnoxious child has ruined the pleasure of dining for you? Ever been at the movies where a rambunctious child talked, spilled his drink or kicked your seat back—ruining your enjoyment of the show?"

Slowly he nodded. "But Mollie—"

"It has little to do with Mollie and more to do with her father and his permitting her to behave that way," she interrupted.

Leaning back in his chair, he scowled at her.

"She's just a little girl," he said again.

"Get over it, Patrick. She's tiny compared to you, but then most people will be, you're so tall. I'm not saying act harshly toward her, just show her the right way to behave."

"Her mother and I didn't get on at the end. Hell, we didn't get on from the day we returned from the honeymoon, I think. We divorced right after Mollie was born and Sylvia got custody. So I didn't see much of her until last year when her mother died and she came to live with me. Mollie's special. And with her mother gone, I'm trying to make it up to her."

"She's your daughter. She needs to know you love her." For a moment, Shelby wished her father had felt the same, had defied her grandmother, stayed to fight the charge and been there for her while she was grow-ing up.

"And part of that caring is raising her to know how to behave. You'll do more harm if she doesn't have any acceptable manners."

"I won't tolerate interference with how I raise my daughter," he said.

"Look, Patrick, I've had time to think this over and it was a dumb idea in the first place. Even dumber if you think I'm going to live in your house and ignore her behavior. Let me pay for breakfast and we'll call it quits," she said.

He looked at her in surprise.

For a moment Patrick felt a touch of panic. He hadn't been sure he wanted to agree with Shelby's crazy plan, but it did buy him time to find a more permanent arrangement for Mollie. If he did agree to the scheme, he'd have someone to help with Mollie— at least until she was enrolled in school. By then, maybe he could rearrange his own work schedule to be available during the afternoon. Or use the after-school day care. He'd figure it out. This marriage bought him some time. And enabled him to keep his daughter.

But to do that, he needed Shelby to follow through with her suggestion.

He looked over at Mollie. She was playing alone on one of the crawl toys the kiddy center provided. She had difficulty relating to the other children at the day care centers and the preschools he'd tried. She *was* wild and undisciplined. But she was so little, and so adorable. And he loved her more than life itself.

He couldn't let her grandmother take her. He'd miss her too much. He wanted to be there for her, see her grow up, hear about the exciting things she learned in school, even mop up tears when some punk boy hurt her as a teenager.

But if he didn't take advantage of Shelby's offer, he was at his wits' end on what to do.

"For the duration of our mock marriage, she'll be your daughter. I don't abide spanking, but I'll listen to your suggestions," he said heavily.

Surprised by Shelby's startled look, he wondered what she thought of him. Would she have even considered talking with him if she didn't need his skill to locate her father?

For the first time he really looked at Shelby. She was pretty in a quiet, unassuming way. Her deep auburn hair was pulled back, then curled around and beneath the bow she wore. Her bright blue eyes were guileless, always meeting his directly, hiding nothing. She was quiet and reserved in a manner as unlike his ex-wife Sylvia as anyone could be. Maybe it wouldn't be all bad working together for a few months.

"I can't devote full-time investigation to your father," he said suddenly, wanting to be up-front with her. "This arrangement will help me out, but I also need cases that will pay hard cash. I'll do the best I can to expedite the search."

"I understand."

"Of course I'm always juggling a dozen or more at a time, so what's one more? And I have a couple of operatives who are skilled in different areas, I'll also assign them to some of the background work."

"Someone needs to talk with Edith Strong."

"Who's Edith Strong?"

"She knew my parents. She was a contemporary of

my grandmother's and may know some specific information about my father. She's the one, besides grandmother, who finally told us the truth about my father's
leaving.''

''Then interviewing her will be a high number on
the list of things to do,'' Patrick said.

''So, we're on?'' she asked.

''I'm in if you are. Mollie starts kindergarten in the
fall. If we stay together until then, I should be able to
locate your father and find suitable after school care
for her.''

She cleared her throat, toying with the napkin on the
table. ''Actually, it would have to be a bit longer—
until my sister Margot has her baby in November.''

He nodded. ''Okay.''

''When do you want to get married?''

''Tomorrow,'' he said dryly.

''What?''

Smiling at her astonishment, Patrick felt a huge
weight disappear. She was still hanging in there. For
the first time he was glad he had not found a boyfriend
in the background who would object to her bizarre suggestion.

Though he didn't understand the other men in
Louisiana. Shelby might be quiet, but she was pretty.
Why hadn't she been married long before—to some
guy who still believed in love and all that stuff?

''I want to get Mollie into the day care as soon as
possible. You set the date,'' he said.

''You're right. You need her taken care of. Get her
established in a normal routine. I don't mind getting
married soon.'' She bit her lip, as a sudden thought hit.

''What?'' he asked. Would he always be able to read

this woman who would soon be his wife? Unlikely, he'd never been able to understand Sylvia.

"I'd say we could elope, but my sisters would never forgive me. Especially Margot. She and her husband eloped a few years ago and then renewed their vows earlier this month with a full church ceremony. She puts a lot of stock in tradition."

"Not that. I've been there. This is not going to turn into a multimedia circus event to keep your sisters from suspecting anything."

"Of course not. I wouldn't want to spend the money on something so frivolous unless this was a real marriage. But we have to do something or they will suspect something is wrong. And then Margot would worry, and try to protect me when she needs to concentrate on delivering a healthy baby."

"We'll do what your sister did—elope and tell them we plan a formal ceremony later."

Shelby shook her head. "No. Margot would fret and I can't have that."

"Are you expecting that our entire marriage will be dictated by your sister whom I've never even met?"

"You can meet her tomorrow. She's invited us to her place for dinner."

"When was this?"

"Last night, before you called. I didn't know if you'd say yes or not to this bizarre arrangement, but thought I should set the stage—just in case."

"Just how did you set this stage?" he asked suspiciously.

Shelby told him and by the time she'd finished, Mollie appeared at her dad's side.

"I want to go," she said, eyeing Shelby cautiously.

"Shelby and I haven't finished talking," Patrick said.

"Isn't there a park nearby? I thought we passed one just a few blocks back," Shelby suggested. "That'd be fun, wouldn't it Mollie? You can play on the swings while your Daddy and I finish our discussion."

The little girl nodded warily.

Settled on a park bench a short time later, Shelby waited while Patrick went over the rules of where Mollie could go and where she couldn't. She enjoyed watching him with his daughter—sometimes thinking she could almost imagine herself with her father twenty years ago.

"Ground rules," Patrick said, joining her on the bench.

"Right. But I know we'll still need to watch her. What else did you want to discuss?"

"You'll move into my place to be there to take of Mollie. It's not big, but we have a third bedroom. Do you want to move your own bed in, or use the Hide-A-Bed that's already there?"

"I'd prefer my own bed," she said. Suddenly the knowledge she'd have to give up her apartment hit her.

"My apartment."

"What about it?"

"I don't want to lose it."

"Sublet it."

Biting her lip in indecision, Shelby didn't know if that would work. "How long do you think this will take?"

"I would expect to find as much as I can in the next few months. We may get lucky and it will only take a few weeks. But I've agreed to stay your husband until your sister has her baby. Or, if I don't find your father by then, we'll just extend the arrangement until I do locate him.''

Five months? She'd spend nearly five months of her life with this disturbing, intriguing man? See him at the breakfast table, cook dinner for him, temporarily share in the raising of his daughter? Live in his home?

Would she enjoy it, or find herself floundering and wishing she knew better how to interact with men? Like this morning—obviously she had not brought up the situation of discipline in a very positive light.

Maybe she could ask Margot for some pointers. Rand seemed totally devoted to her.

Of course, he loved her sister.

What would it be like to fall madly in love with a man? To expect kisses morning and night, to share a room, a bed?

Head surged through her again. Quickly averting her eyes, she tried to bring her wayward thoughts under control.

She wasn't going into this with any thought of falling for Patrick.

And she had no worry he'd fall for her. Not after his tirade on marriage and the scathing tone in his voice when he spoke about his first wife.

This was a business proposition. Nothing more!

''I'll sublet. Move my furniture into your place. I'll do the cooking and the laundry. Can you do the vacuuming and picking up?''

He nodded. ''I'm used to doing it all, so to have you do the cooking is worth your weight in gold. Especially if you are as good as you say.''

''Oh, I am.''

For a moment she saw a flash of deeper interest in Patrick's eyes. But he quickly turned away, searching the playing children until he located Mollie.

"I can contribute equally to the family coffers," she said into the silence.

He glared at her. "I can afford to support my own family."

"True, but this is different. Since I work, I can contribute. I insist on paying my own expenses."

"You're doing a lot by providing the day care."

"Do you know what some of your competition was going to charge me, had I been able to afford it?"

"No." Gazing into her eyes, Patrick's pique faded. He didn't know about the competition and didn't care. Suddenly he wanted to know more about Shelby Beaufort—more than what he'd found for the preliminary report he'd compiled. The surface information was easily obtained. But he was curious about what lay beneath. She puzzled him, and he loved solving puzzles.

Not that he'd let his interest carry him away. He'd learned his lesson when married to Sylvia. No more entanglements with women. Actually, Shelby was doing him a favor, by providing a solid barrier against other females who thought they could captivate his attention.

She looked at him expectantly.

"What?" he said.

"I asked about your getting a new secretary."

"I haven't found one yet. Why?"

"Maybe I could help out in the evenings if you still need help. Organization is my thing."

"I noticed that from your personnel records. You've received a lot of commendations."

"And just how did you get into them?"

"I told your supervisor I was doing a high-level security investigation and she showed them to me."

"All of them?"

"Just the glowing commendations, the praises for the innovative techniques that saved time and money and made reporting easier, and the hefty raises you've received over the years. You should be proud of yourself doing so well in a predominantly man's field."

She bristled, but held her tongue. "One day I'm going to return the favor," she said.

He laughed. "Don't be like all the other women I know who think being a private investigator is exciting and romantic. Most of it is a lot of researching records and files. Or sitting in a car waiting for someone to do something stupid."

"It's not dangerous, is it?"

"Not the field I specialize in. You're thinking of TV shows, or the movies. Those private detectives are practically supermen."

She nodded. "My offer still stands."

Patrick studied her for a moment. "Thanks. I might need the help if I can't find someone soon. Back to this marriage, are you sure we can't elope?"

"I'm positive. But it doesn't have to be an elaborate wedding. In fact the more low-key we keep it the better. But I will want my sisters there and you must have one or two friends who should come for appearance sake."

"I have a couple." She was right, the fewer who knew the real truth surrounding their marriage, the fewer explanations they'd have to come up with when they ended it.

Shelby glanced at Mollie. "I wonder if we could do everything next Saturday?" she asked.

"Depending upon what you mean by everything. A simple ceremony before a judge shouldn't be that complicated. You're the one who would want the fancy dress and other folderols."

"I can buy a dress in a day or two. So next Saturday suits you?"

"Yeah." He stretched his long legs out and leaned back in the bench, slipping his fingers in the tops of his pockets. "I can't believe I'm doing this," he said watching Mollie play.

"If you'd rather not—"

"No, it'll work. I'll see to it."

Shelby nodded. She'd added her own vow, she'd do her best for them both and at the end she'd have the information she wanted about her father.

CHAPTER THREE

SHELBY stared at the house, butterflies kickboxing in her stomach. Nervous, she tried deep breathing, then feared she'd hyperventilate. She *could* do this, she repeated, wondering if she was fooling herself.

Though lying had never been a strong suit of hers, surely she could convince her sister, and Rand, that she and the man beside her were madly in love and couldn't wait to get married.

The man beside her.

She looked at him. Meeting his gaze, she was startled by the amusement in his eyes.

"I don't think this is funny," she said.

"You look as if you're going to an execution. Relax. I thought you liked your sister."

"I do. I love her. But what if she suspects this isn't a normal marriage? If I can't convince her, she'll worry and that's definitely not something I want happening."

Patrick shrugged. "I've worked undercover before. You imagine the part, then step in. Didn't you ever do plays or something when in school?"

"No." She'd been too shy.

"Well, it's easy. Just go along with the role you've created."

She nodded and took another deep breath.

"Of course, you understand props. We need props to make it work."

Swinging her gaze at him again she shook her head. "What props?"

"This for one."

Patrick leaned over and kissed her soundly on her surprised mouth.

It wasn't just a light brushing of lips but a full-blown kiss. Shelby's eyes widened, then slowly drifted close as her senses kicked in and became embroiled with the sensations that suddenly crowded inside.

Her heart raced, the butterflies forgotten as heat crashed through her like the hottest Louisiana sunshine. When he pulled back, she slowly opened her eyes and stared at him in bemusement.

"Better," he said, running his hands through her hair, mussing it up.

"Stop, what are you doing?"

"Setting the stage. You want your sister to believe we're in love, right?"

Shelby thought she did, but with the blood pounding through her veins and the echo of thunder in her ears from his kiss, she was having trouble thinking at all!

"At least wait until there's an audience," Shelby said, opening the screeching door.

Patrick got out and swung around the front of his car to catch up with her quick walk up the walkway. He hadn't expected anything from that kiss—just to tease her into a better frame of mind. Now, he wondered what had hit him. And would it happen again if he kissed her a second time?

Shelby rang the doorbell as Patrick joined her on the wide wooden porch. Glancing around she looked everywhere but at him.

"Chill out, babe. It was only a kiss."

At that her gaze snapped up at him. "Don't call me babe!"

Patrick smiled and leaned closer—so close Shelby could breathe his scent, that tangy spicy aftershave and the unique scent that was Patrick's alone—male and magical. She swallowed hard and tried to ignore the fluttering of her heart. This was make-believe—nothing more.

"Think of it as a term of affection."

"It brings to mind tight skirts and slinky women."

"Ah, now that's an interesting image." His gaze ran down the length of her and Shelby was hard pressed not to turn around and storm back to the car. Maybe coming tonight had been a mistake. He wasn't touching her, yet she felt every inch come alive. She wanted to push him away, rail against the unfairness of the situation—he was deliberately provoking her and she had no way to retaliate.

"Maybe we should explore this a bit more—word association. If babe brings slinky women to mind, what do you think about when I say hot as honey?"

Shelby drew herself up and tightened her lips. "Will you behave? We are here to make sure Margot and Rand believe we are madly in love. Provoking me isn't the way to prove that!"

"Prove what?" Margot opened the door and looked from her sister's angry gaze to the amusement dancing in the eyes of the man standing next to her. Slowly she smiled.

"You must be Patrick," she said, holding out a hand.

"And you're Margot." He shook her hand and ushered Shelby into the cool house, his hand warm on her lower back.

Shelby forced a smile, kissing Margot's cheek. "Yes, this is Patrick."

"Annoyed, are you?" Margot asked, her own smile wide and amused.

"He's enough to drive a saint to do something crazy."

"And I never even *pretended* to be a *saint*," Patrick said.

"Come and meet my husband," Margot said, walking down the wide hallway toward a large room in the back. Windows covered one wall, bringing the lovely garden into the room.

Shelby wished she'd come up with some other way to have Margot be assured about what she was doing. But now that they were here, she'd have to make the most of it.

Rand turned to her after greeting Patrick and kissed her lightly on the cheek. His eyes missed nothing, from her heightened color to the mussed hair Patrick had tousled. He sought Margot and they shared a look.

Shelby refused to be annoyed. At least she was over her stage fright.

Until Patrick placed his arm across her shoulders and walked her to the sofa. Sitting much too close, he settled right beside her. She would have scooted away, if he'd let her. His leg pressed against hers, his arm encircled her shoulders. She felt surrounded, crowded. Aware.

Toying with her hair, Patrick calmly answered Rand's questions and Margot's gentle probing. But Shelby couldn't concentrate. Her entire being was caught up in the emotions that raced through her. His casual attention touched something deep inside.

Surprised, she found she liked it. And that scared her. She was not a woman to be attracted to some man just because he made a play for her. And in this case, Patrick was almost ignoring her. Yet she couldn't shake the awareness that grew with each second.

"I made shrimp Creole," Margot said. "Want to help me with the last bit?"

Shelby nodded and jumped up. Suddenly realizing that would mean leaving Patrick alone with Rand, she hesitated. "Will you be all right here?" she asked softly.

He nodded. "I think I can defend myself until you return."

Once in the huge old-fashioned kitchen, Margot peeked around the door one last time then rounded on her sister.

"He's amazing. And obviously crazy about you— he can't keep his hands off. Where did you find him?"

"I told you, he sometimes works for my company. Doing investigations, that kind of thing." Trying to remember her own role, she smiled and wondered if it looked dreamy or just spaced out. "He's wonderful, isn't he? You do like him, right?"

"So far." Margot narrowed her eyes. "Just how involved are you?"

Shelby took a deep breath and prayed this would work. "Involved enough to invite you to our wedding!"

"Wow!" Margot hugged her. "I can't believe it. Does Georgia know?"

"Not yet. I wanted to make sure you met him and liked him. But I'll call her when I get home."

"Nope, we'll call now. She'd never forget us if we left her out. Rand!" Margot went to the door. "Do we have any champagne? We're celebrating! Did you know Patrick and Shelby are engaged?"

She whirled around without waiting for an answer and hurried across the kitchen. "So when will you get married? Christmas is so lovely. But June is a wonderful month, too."

"Actually, we thought about June as well—but this year, not next. Are you free next Saturday?"

Margot stopped and turned to look at her sister.

"Next Saturday?"

Shelby wished she'd waited to tell that bit of news. Margot looked stunned. Maybe the entire idea was bad to begin with. "Are you all right? Should you sit down?"

"I'm fine. Stunned, but fine. Why the rush?"

Shelby shrugged. "I don't want a big wedding. So why not get married right away? I mean we talked it over and both want to, so why not just do it and then…move…in…together." It sounded weak. Or was it her guilty conscience talking? She wasn't sure. Wishing Margot would at least look happy again, she wondered what else she could add to convince her sister this was a good idea.

Rand walked into the kitchen, followed by Patrick.

"I guess you told her, huh?" he said.

Shelby nodded as Rand crossed to the refrigerator and rummaged in it for a tall bottle of champagne.

"How do you think she's taking it?" she whispered, watching her sister.

Patrick leaned over and kissed her, then held her chin with his hand. "I'd say your sister is going to need a bit of time to get used to this." Looking directly at Margot, he raised an eyebrow. "Right?"

"To say the least. Congratulations. But next Saturday?"

"We don't want to wait," he said.

"Is there any reason for the rush? I mean, another week or two. Or month or two. Just so you both can be sure."

Rand opened the bottle with a loud pop. Quickly filling three glasses, he handed one to Patrick and to Shelby. "Sorry, darling, you'll have to have water. But you can still join in the toast."

"Rand, they are talking about getting married this next Saturday—six days from now."

He slipped his arm around her waist and drew her close. "You can't remember back six years? We didn't want to wait, either."

"I guess."

Shelby knew she should say something to convince her sister, but she was tongue tied. It was all moving too fast. Everything seemed to be spinning out of control—not the least of which was the way her senses went haywire the minute Patrick touched her. Could he feel it?

He clinked his glass against hers and sipped the sparkling beverage. She drank a gulp and her eyes watered with the sudden burst of bubbles. At her exclamation, Patrick brushed his lips across hers, winking at her look of astonishment.

With wobbly knees, Shelby leaned against him, wishing she could get him away from her sister long enough to deliver a blistering sermon on why he had to stop kissing her!

"If you two are sure, who are we to second-guess you?" Margot said. "Let's call Georgia."

Shelby smiled and nodded. Relief hit her. Margot suspected nothing, and would not worry. Glancing at Patrick, she swallowed. Maybe Margot wouldn't worry, but suddenly Shelby wondered what she thought she was doing—marrying a total stranger who affected her as no one else ever had.

"That went well, don't you think?" Patrick asked three hours later when he opened the passenger door for Shelby. Rand and Margot remained on the porch, illuminated by the overhead light. Waving once more, Shelby climbed in and winced when the door gave its usual loud screech.

"Wouldn't oil fix that problem?" she asked when Patrick slid in behind the wheel a moment later.

"What problem?"

"The door and the awful noise it makes!" she said, knowing she was looking for something to vent her frustration on. She refused to give voice to the uncertainties that plagued her. The door might as well take the brunt of her emotions.

Patrick started the car and smoothly pulled out into the street. "I'll see about oiling it tomorrow," he said.

Annoyed he'd given in so easily, she frowned and stared out through the windshield.

"Anything else?" he asked in a bland voice.

She flicked him a look. "Like what?"

"I don't know, that's why I'm asking. I can't read

minds. But I can read body language, and you are up-tight about something. What?''

Shelby opened her mouth to tell him, then snapped it shut. She wasn't sure she even knew what had her so upset. It had to do with the kisses he'd given her, and the feelings that churned inside her and the uncertainty about what she was planning.

"You've been this way since we arrived at your sister's," Patrick added.

"Well, you didn't help matters."

"What?"

"Fiddling with my hair, putting your arm on my shoulders, kissing me." She smoothed the material of her skirt, tracing the material with a fingertip.

"And here I thought we handled the romantic setting well. That's what people do who are in love. Thought we were trying to convince your sister and her husband."

Shelby nodded. She was being silly, she knew. But she had never expected the wash of awareness and attraction that flooded through her just being near Patrick. She couldn't afford to let herself become enamored with the man. They had a business agreement. And she had to stick to her part of the bargain if she wanted him to stick to his.

And she did. Wistfully she gazed back out the window. She'd so wanted to find out about her father. Wouldn't her old-family conscious grandmother have a fit to know Shelby hadn't considered the Beauforts the be-all and end-all of families? She yearned to know about her Williams side.

"Shelby?"

"What?" She blinked and looked at Patrick.

"I lost you for a moment. We were talking about acting like we were lovers at your sister's."

Acting like lovers. The image that sprang to mind was not easily banished. Shelby stared at Patrick in the sporadic light from other vehicles as he drove. He was not handsome in a traditional sense, but strong and masculine and quite fascinating.

What would it be like to be lovers?

She had never fallen in love, never made love. But for a moment she wondered what it would be like with Patrick. He made her feel different—on the edge of something thrilling. He gave her a heightened awareness of the potential between a man and a woman.

She cleared her throat. "I guess you just did what you thought was necessary to project that image."

"Would you have had us behave as mere acquaintances?"

"I guess not. It was just so unexpected."

"Why? I told you I would act the part. I'm good at undercover activities."

She couldn't tell him the unexpected aspect had to do with her own reaction to his kisses.

"I'll remember that."

"Are we going to spend a lot of time with Margot and Rand? Or your sister Georgia?"

"No, why?"

"Just wondered how often we'd have to play this game."

Of course, without the audience they had to convince, there would be no reason for kisses and caresses.

"Well, there will be some occasions," she hedged. While she didn't think she could remain impervious to his touch, neither was she willing to forego the pleasure entirely in the future—if she could come up with a reason to indulge.

Good grief, was she losing her mind?

"We will see them next Saturday at the wedding, and then I can make excuses for a while, which will buy some time. They'll expect us to want to be alone for a while. So you won't have to draw on your powers of subterfuge."

"I wasn't complaining." He reached out and captured one of her hands, linking his fingers through hers and resting them on one muscular thigh. Shelby caught her breath, aware of the tingle of awareness that shimmered through her at the intimacy of his touch, of their linked hands. "I liked it. Didn't you?"

She mumbled something, once again caught up in the whirlwind of sensations that seemed to short-circuit her brain.

"I liked your sister and her husband. They almost make a man believe in marriage."

"What?"

"My own experience wasn't so hot, but watching them is like peering into a private lovefest. He obviously adores her and she hangs on his every word with matching adoration in her every glance. Haven't they been married for a while?"

"Yes and no," Shelby said slowly.

Patrick glanced at her, tightening his grip on her hand briefly. "You're good at that—ambiguous answers. They either have or they haven't. Right?"

"They've been married over six years, but only lived together for a few months, then were separated for five years. They got back together this spring."

"The reason for the separation?"

"The miscarriage started it, but my grandmother perpetuated it," Shelby said shortly.

"Ah, the same grandmother who drove your father away. She sounds like a real charmer. Sorry I missed getting to meet her."

"I suspect you would have given her a run for her money."

"We'll find your father, that will be the best revenge," he said with another friendly squeeze on her hand.

"So after Saturday, you won't have to pretend to be in love for a while," Shelby said, more to remind herself than to tell Patrick. "Do you want me to get Mollie a dress for the wedding?"

"Good luck. The kid doesn't wear dresses."

"Why not?"

"Shorts are good for play, and the last time I tried to get her into a dress she threw a hissy fit, so I haven't tried again. She, uh, might not want to come without her hat."

"Does she sleep with it?"

"No, but she wears it all the time when she's not asleep."

"Why?"

"I don't know—she likes it."

"Well, prevail upon her to forego it for one day. I would think a little girl would love to dress up for a special outing."

Patrick shook his head. "I don't know, Shelby. Maybe we should just let her wear shorts."

"I could come over Wednesday night and take her to the store and see if we could find something for her."

He was silent for a moment, then shrugged. "Fine with me. I'll take us out to dinner and then we'll see how it goes."

He pulled in to the curb and stopped in front of Shelby's apartment.

"No need to get out. I'll be fine," she said brightly.

"No problem." He stopped the car and got out, going around to open her door.

Shelby didn't wince at the screech this time. Was she beginning to get used to it? Silently they took the elevator to her floor and walked down the quiet hall. Stopping by her door, she fished out her keys.

"Thanks for going," she said, fumbling with the lock.

Patrick's hand covered hers, guiding in the key and turning it.

"I enjoyed meeting Margot and Rand. Are you all right?"

Shelby nodded and smiled brightly. "Sure."

"You seem nervous. You did pretty good with the pretense, except you seemed startled every time I touched you."

"Well—"

"Maybe all you need is practice."

"What?"

"You know the old saying, practice makes perfect."

With that, he covered her mouth with his.

Shelby was breathing hard when he lifted his head and gazed down at her, his expression giving nothing away.

"Better. See, practice does make perfect."

"Good night, Patrick," she said and flew through the door, closing it in his face. Her knees felt wobbly and her heart raced. She could still feel the wonderful imprint of his lips against hers. Instead of acting like a scared schoolgirl, she should have pretended to have a certain level of sophistication and kissed him back.

Leaning against the door, she sighed. She did need more practice if she was to pull this off and not give rise to speculation about how his kisses affected her. Just how much would be enough?

She could hardly wait until Wednesday!

CHAPTER FOUR

SHELBY was surprised at the anticipation that built as
Wednesday afternoon progressed. Patrick had called
that morning to say he'd pick her up at six. Never a
clock watcher, Shelby seemed to check the time every
ten minutes. Giving in to the excitement, she left work
early and hurried home to change into something more
suitable for shopping than her business suit and heels.

Patrick had reiterated the invitation to dinner, and
she wondered where they would go? Another fast food
place for Mollie, or a family restaurant?

Wearing a loose, gauzy sundress and sandals, Shelby
was ready when the doorbell rang. From the incessant
sound, she knew Mollie was the one pushing the button.

"Hi," Shelby opened the door and caught her
breath. She hadn't seen Patrick since Sunday. Why did
looking into his eyes cause her heart to jump and then
pound? Forcing her gaze down, she smiled at Mollie.

"Hi, Mollie, ready to go shopping?"

The little girl leaned against her father's leg and
shook her head. Her shorts and shirt were neat and
clean. The cap sat squarely on her head.

"Don't gots to."

"Don't have to," Shelby corrected gently. "But it
would be a lot of fun. We can buy you a pretty dress
to wear on Saturday, and maybe shiny shoes."

Mollie watched her warily and shook her head,

clutching her teddy bear tightly. Her baseball cap shadowed her face, but Shelby caught the stubborn pout.

Patrick picked her up and looked at Shelby. She saw the family resemblance, and the family solidarity. Hadn't they worked things out yet?

"Ready to eat?" Patrick asked.

"I am." Shelby slipped her keys into her purse and slung it over one shoulder. Pulling the door shut, she tested it to make sure it was locked. "Where are we going?"

"There's a nice place near the Quarter that's fine for kids. Then we'll be close to some of the department stores on Canal Street."

The place Patrick chose was perfect for families. It was early enough to be uncrowded.

Shelby made small talk until they ordered. The restaurant provided crayons and a black-and-white menu for children with a scene for them to color. Mollie began industriously coloring in the background with bright blue.

"Any place special you shop for her clothes?"

"No. I've only had her for a year. Some of the clothes her mother bought still fit. And we've not had the occasion to buy fancy dresses. Besides, she hates to shop."

Shelby looked at the little girl, then her father. "Does she, or is it you?"

Patrick glanced at Mollie. "I'm not so thrilled with it. Do you know how tiny the buttons are on kids' clothes?"

Hiding a smile, Shelby nodded. "Maybe it will be easier with the two of us. I promise to fasten all the tiny buttons."

"Most of the time shorts and a shirt are enough."

"But not at a wedding," Shelby said firmly.

"Speaking of which, did you arrange it?"

She nodded. "At noon, at the courthouse. Judge Thompson. It will only take a few minutes and then we can go to lunch. Georgia and Margot insist I have to stay with Margot Friday night and have Rand give me away."

Patrick looked at her. "You're not wearing some fancy white dress with a veil and big bouquet of roses, are you?"

"I could," she said.

He closed his eyes. "I thought this was going to be a small wedding, in and out, so to speak."

Laughing softly, Shelby reached out and patted his arm, snatching her hand back when she realized what she'd done. "It will be. I have a nice white suit and a skimpy hat with a tiny veil. Maybe you'll give me a corsage or something."

"Yeah, that sounds great. Lunch and then we're done, right?"

She nodded, feeling a pang with the thought of the ceremony. Once upon a time she had thought she'd find a wonderful man to marry and raise a family with. There was still the possibility, but this would be her first wedding. And for her sisters' sake, she had to make it seem as real as possible.

"You're not expecting a honeymoon, are you?" he asked.

"No."

He looked relieved. Shelby wondered what he really thought about this crazy plan.

"In fact, Patrick, except for the few times you and

I have to be with my family, you can continue to live your life just as you always do. I don't plan to interfere.''

"For the last year, my life's been pretty much tied up with Mollie.''

"Before that?''

"Before that, Sylvia had custody and wasn't really generous with allowing me time to see her. Something always seemed to come up at the last moment.''

"That must have been hard. You two seem perfect together.''

He nodded.

Shelby waited for him to say more, but he didn't. She glanced at Mollie. The picture on the menu was almost fully colored. She hoped the meal arrived soon. She was running out of things to say.

"Look, Daddy, I'm coloring good.'' Mollie held up the picture. Scribbles ran over all the lines. Shelby didn't think she remembered seeing a green elephant before.

"Wonderful, Mollie. I like your picture.'' Patrick's tone was sincere and full of love.

Watching them, Shelby's heart melted. He was so obviously proud of his daughter it warmed her from head to toe. How much she'd missed in her own life by not having her parents.

"Show Shelby.''

"Don't gots to,'' Mollie said slapping the picture down on the table and frowning at Shelby.

"I can see it from here. It's pretty,'' she said, refusing to be hurt by the child's actions.

"Turn the sheet over, baby, and draw a new picture

on the back,'' Patrick suggested with an apologetic glance at Shelby.

Once Mollie was again engrossed in coloring, Shelby shrugged. ''It's all right if she doesn't warm up right away. From what you've said, she's had a lot of different people in her life over the last year. She's probably protecting herself by not getting too friendly until she knows if I'll be around for a while or not.''

Once again, Shelby began to question the wisdom of her plan. It seemed straightforward when she'd first voiced it. She'd help Patrick, he'd help her. But Mollie was an unknown in the equation. What would this arrangement do to her?

Dinner went well. Shelby wondered if Patrick had a talk with Mollie before they came to the restaurant. She was the model of propriety. When Shelby commented on it, Patrick smiled smugly.

''So, tell me, how did you manage? Quite a difference from the donut place.''

''Told her she could bring her bear.''

''The teddy bear?''

He nodded. ''Usually I don't let her bring him everywhere with her. She's old enough to go out in public without it. But I let her bring him on the condition that she was a very good girl.''

''Bribery.''

He nodded smugly. ''Works every time.''

''I'll remember that.''

He looked into her eyes, his narrowing slightly. ''You do that.''

When they finished eating, Shelby suggested they try one of the major department stores on Canal Street. The childrens' department was large and offered a wide variety of clothes. She found two dresses immediately that she thought would be appropriate for Mollie.

"Which one do you like?" she asked the little girl.

Mollie had retreated to her dad's side and looked at the dresses suspiciously.

"I like the blue one," Patrick said nudging his daughter.

"I like both the blue and the pink. Which do you like, Mollie?" Shelby asked again.

Mollie pointed to the blue one.

"Let's go try it on, shall we?" Shelby asked, replacing the pink one on the rack.

"Don't gots to," Mollie said, clutching her bear tighter.

"Don't have to," Shelby corrected. "Don't say got, Mollie, say have. And I think you'll look very pretty in this dress. You can try it on and show your daddy. Want to?"

Mollie shook her head.

Shelby looked at Patrick for help, but he just watched her with amused interest.

Frustrated, she knew this was some kind of test. But she hadn't a clue how to deal with children. Spotting the teddy bear, she had an idea.

"I tell you what, Mollie. Let's try on the dress to see if it fits and then we'll go find something pretty for your teddy bear. So he'll be all dressed up at the wedding, too."

"Bribery," Patrick murmured.

"Okay," Mollie said, relinquishing her hold on her father's leg and holding out her hand for Shelby's.

"Whatever works," Shelby said triumphantly.

The sound of Patrick's laughter followed them to the

dressing rooms. Once there Shelby had another minor skirmish in getting Mollie to remove her hat. When she saw the chopped-off hair, Shelby began to understand why Mollie wanted to wear her hat all the time.

She looked adorable in the dress, despite the baseball cap she'd insisted in putting on once the dress was buttoned.

"Go show your daddy how pretty you look," Shelby said with a smile.

When Mollie darted from the stall, Shelby picked up the bear, wondering where they could find clothes for him. He was a bit ragged, obviously from years of loving.

Mollie rushed back in, her face smiling. "Daddy said I look like a fairy princess."

"And so you do. We'll take the dress home and you can wear it on Saturday."

Mollie pirouetted before the mirror for several minutes before allowing Shelby to unfasten and remove the dress. Once again wearing her shorts, shirt and baseball cap, they left to find Patrick.

As they waited for the clerk to ring up the sale, Shelby moved near Patrick.

"Where does Mollie get her hair cut?" she asked softly.

He looked guilty. "I do it. She hates barber shops."

"Barber shops? Patrick, she should go to a salon that caters for children."

He looked at her for a long moment, then nodded. "You were right at the beginning. I do need a wife. You can take her there, buy her clothes, and do all the things for a little girl that I don't have a clue about."

"Your daughter looks darling in the dress," the sales clerk told Shelby.

She started to correct the woman, then just smiled. In only a few days, technically Mollie would be her stepdaughter. For a moment Shelby tried to consider all the changes she'd find in her life. It seemed like a lot all at once. But she couldn't lose sight of the reason for it.

For a moment she let herself imagine marrying forever. To bind her life with Patrick's. Maybe they'd have children of their own. Soon outgrow his house and need a larger one. Nothing as ostentatious or cold as Beaufort Hall had been, but a big house full of laughter and love.

"Ready?" Patrick said, shattering the daydream.

"Sure. We need to find something for the bear." Daydreams had no place in this arrangement. It was a business deal, pure and simple.

Luck was with them, Shelby felt, when they found a cute vest and top hat with a little elastic chin strap for the bear. Mollie was ecstatic and carefully carried her bear proudly.

"Now if we can get her hair trimmed, we'll be all set," Shelby said. It was getting late. "When does Mollie go to bed?"

"Usually around eight. But since there's no place for her to go tomorrow, she can sleep in. Think you can find a place this late?"

"No. But I'll call around first thing in the morning. Can you take her?"

"Of course. She comes with me to the office each day, but we're not there long. She gets bored, or into mischief."

"Did you find another secretary?"

"Not yet. But I have a temp in who can at least answer the phones and do some rudimentary typing. Your offer to help still open?"

Shelby nodded.

"Maybe next week I might have to take you up on it. Or with my being in the office without Mollie, maybe I can instruct the temp enough to get caught up."

"I've told Personnel about my marriage and already preregistered Mollie for the day care starting on Monday."

"I've already assigned one of my operatives to canvass the fifty states looking for a birth record for your father. We have his name and age—we'll find him."

Shelby nodded, pleased that Patrick had already started the ball rolling in locating her father even before the wedding. What if he found him almost immediately? She was committed to this marriage at least until Margot delivered.

Patrick dropped Shelby at home, but refused her invitation to come up for coffee. He had to get Mollie home and into bed.

When Shelby let herself into her apartment, she was surprised to find the lights on.

"Hello?"

"Hey, Shelby. Where have you been?" Georgia was lounging on the sofa, watching TV. She sprang up when her sister entered the living room. "I let myself in when you didn't answer the bell."

"I didn't know you were coming over," Shelby said, giving her sister a brief hug.

"Out with Patrick?" Georgia guessed, her eyes twinkling.

"Yes, we went to dinner."

"I guess that answers one question," Georgia said, turning to cut off the TV.

"What question?" Shelby asked, tossing her purse on a chair and sinking down in another. She was tired. How long was Georgia planning to stay?

"Whether you and Patrick are sleeping together already."

Heat stole into her cheeks. Shelby tried to look indignant, but the image that danced before her eyes made that difficult.

"No, we are not!" she said. The feelings that swamped her couldn't be disappointment. She hardly knew the man. Certainly not enough to sleep with him! Though, of course, her sisters didn't know that. They thought she and Patrick were wildly in love and impatient to be married.

"You needn't sound so indignant. Engaged people do sometimes anticipate the marriage vows. Anyway, I'm glad I don't have to dash out in order to avoid being a fifth wheel. But I'm sorry I didn't get to meet him. Margot said he's very tall and has a great sense of humor. But we're both surprised at the suddenness of it all."

"I am, too, if you want the truth." But not the entire truth, of course, Shelby thought. She had to keep the pretense for Georgia as well as Margot. Her sister often thought before she spoke and Shelby didn't want to take the chance Georgia would spill the beans to Margot and cause her sister to worry.

"But you're sure?" Georgia pressed, looking serious.

"I'm sure." Shelby said with conviction. It was an arrangement that could only be beneficial. Patrick would keep Mollie, so the little girl would not have to grow up without a father. And sooner or later Patrick would locate Sam Williams, of that Shelby was certain. If he attacked his cases as he did his personal life, she knew Patrick would be wildly successful.

"Then the next thing is what can I do to help? I've taken the next three days off from work to help with anything you need."

"Oh, Georgia, you didn't have to do that. But thanks. I think I've got everything lined up, but you know how things can go wrong at the last minute." Shelby explained what she'd done for the ceremony, showed her sister the suit she'd bought for the event and discussed the luncheon reservations she'd made.

Remembering Patrick's adage about playing a role, she tried to include his name in the conversation as often as she could. And each time, she felt her heart skip a beat. The man was positively dangerous—even in absentia. But Georgia seemed convinced of the reality of her sister's devotion for the man. Shelby couldn't wait to tell him. She wanted some of that praise he so freely gave his daughter.

"You haven't said a word about your honeymoon. Where are you going?" Georgia asked some time later.

Shelby froze for a moment. She should have anticipated that question. Especially after her sister and Rand had taken a second honeymoon for a few days after they renewed their vows. And it was tradition.

"Actually, I have taken so much time off dealing

with Grandmother's estate, that I don't have a lot of time left. And Patrick is really busy with a new case, so we've decided to postpone a honeymoon for a while. It will be enough to be together.''

Georgia looked at her suspiciously, but her expression cleared in another moment and she grinned. ''I guess anywhere the two of you are is good enough for a honeymoon, right?''

Shelby nodded.

''And you'll be living in his place, did you say?''

''Yes. We'll be moving most of my things this weekend. I've already started packing.''

''That's no fun. You two go off somewhere and at least spend the weekend together. I have a bunch of friends at the hospital. We'll pack you up and move you. Consider it part of my wedding present.''

Good grief, Shelby thought. Her sister would examine every inch of Patrick's house and know instantly something was wrong if asked to put Shelby's things in a separate bedroom. How could she get out of this?

''I can't let you do that!''

''Nonsense. You can stay at some fancy hotel downtown and just give me the keys to his place. By the time you get there Sunday night, I'll have all your things moved and put away.''

''I'll check with Patrick,'' Shelby stalled. Surely he could come up with a convincing reason to refuse her sister's offer. Panic struck. Shelby obviously wasn't as quick on her feet as Patrick. Came from practice, she was sure. She liked order and organization. Patrick's very life's career dealt in uncertainties, and quick thinking.

Shelby felt exhausted when she went to bed. Georgia

was sleeping on the couch, and planned to stay with her sister until the ceremony. Tomorrow they'd finalize everything and Friday night go to Margot's for the evening. Shelby knew things were spinning out of control, but she couldn't seem to stop them. Not without giving her family a hint of the true nature of this rushed marriage. And that she refused to do.

At work Thursday morning, Shelby located a beauty salon which could take Mollie on a rush basis. She called Patrick. He wasn't at home, so she tried the office.

"O'Shaunnessy." His tone was clipped and professional. Shelby smiled.

"Hi, Patrick. I've got some good news and some bad. Which do you want first?"

"If the bad is you've changed your mind, I don't want to hear it at all. No, Mollie, don't touch that!" The receiver banged on the desk. Shelby waited patiently. In just a moment he spoke again.

"Sorry, she was trying the paper cutter. That's all I'd need, to show up Saturday with a kid minus four fingers."

"My bad news is not that I changed my mind." For a moment she let the knowledge he'd consider that bad to permeate. It was nice. "Actually in other circumstances it might be considered good. But not in this." Quickly she outlined Georgia's suggestion.

"So what's the problem? We'd owe her big-time because we don't have to move the stuff ourselves."

"No! Don't you see, she'll think we are sharing a room and move all my stuff into your bedroom."

"And we can't move it out later?"

"You wouldn't mind the disruption?"

The silence on the other end went on for several seconds. Finally Patrick spoke slowly. "You know, Shelby, we might want to think about this for a bit. A man has needs, just as a woman does. We'll be married."

Stunned, Shelby gripped the receiver. Was he propositioning her?

"Mollie, put that down. Shelby? I've got to cut this short. We can discuss that later. What's the good news?"

"I've found a place that will cut Mollie's hair." Reading the address, Shelby was amazed her voice even worked. She wanted to discuss his odd suggestion now, not at some future date. Wanted to deny all interest. Only, that would be another lie. She found Patrick O'Shaunnessy absolutely fascinating.

While he found her merely convenient for watching his daughter. Backing away from the tantalizing thoughts of making their marriage something more, Shelby tried to get a grip on her emotions. All brides were emotional. This would pass.

"Okay, thanks. I'll take her and if she screams the place down, we'll be sure they have your name!"

Shelby laughed. "She'll be fine. You'll see a world of difference between a beauty parlor and a barber shop. The experience will be good for you."

"I have all the experience I need right now. Anything else?"

"No, I guess not. You have the address and room for the judge."

"Yep, tucked in my wallet. And the new shoes for Mollie, and we'll get dressed early enough that if I can't get the buttons done, I'll go across to my neighbor. It'll make her day to cross-examine me about why Mollie is getting so dressed up,'' he grumbled.

Shelby laughed again. Talking with Patrick was always an adventure. And he was so wonderful with his daughter. Once again, Shelby knew she was doing the right thing to enable the man to keep Mollie with him. That little girl would never lack for love and attention while she was growing up.

''See you Saturday, babe,'' Patrick said as he hung up.

Shelby grimaced as she replaced the receiver. *Babe* again. Was she going to have to cure him of that like she needed to cure Mollie of saying ''gots''?

Saturday was a beautiful day, sunny and warm. Margot prepared a lavish breakfast which she and Georgia served Shelby in bed. Then they both promptly sat on the spread and shared the feast.

''This is like when we were kids,'' Margot said, nibbling on a slice of bread coated with marmalade.

''Yes, only we don't have to worry about Grandmother storming in and ruining everything,'' Georgia said.

''No, she did that long ago when she ran our father off,'' Shelby said.

Margot and Georgia looked at her.

''I vaguely remember him, but you were so young, I didn't think you'd miss him that much,'' Margot said slowly.

''I didn't have to know him to miss him. Remember all the school events when parents attended? Not just the recitals that Grandmother came to, but the soccer events, or the May Day carnival? I was always so envious of girls whose fathers swung them up in their arms and hugged them. I imagined them playing ball, or tag or something in their yards on weekends. Or going on picnics or even just sitting together on a sofa and reading.''

''So it wasn't just me,'' Margot said slowly.

''No, it wasn't,'' Georgia said. ''I would have loved to have both our parents. Once I learned Grandmother was the reason our father left, I couldn't help wondering about Mother. Did she just give up? If Harriet hadn't interfered, would we still have both parents?''

The three sisters were silent for a long moment, until Margot looked around and then smiled brightly. ''Hey, no long faces. We have a wedding to attend today! Aren't you thrilled to death, Shelby?''

Remembering her role, Shelby threw herself into it enthusiastically. Neither sister would ever suspect the true reason. Time enough to explain everything after Margot's baby was safely born and the mock marriage to Patrick had ended.

Dressing in the creamy-white silk suit, Shelby was delighted with the way she looked. Something caused her eyes to sparkle and her skin to glow with subtle color. She sat quietly while Georgia fussed with her hair, pleased with the resulting cascade of curls that looked perfect with the jaunty little hat and veil.

''Here, this was Mother's.'' Margot handed her a locket. ''It's old and borrowed.''

''Here, this is blue.'' Georgia handed her a ruffly garter. ''And I know Patrick will love removing it to toss.''

''Georgia, there are only going to be about six people there. Not enough to fuss with such traditions.''

"If there is one bachelor, that's enough."

When they walked into the living room, Rand rose. Wearing a dark suit with snowy white shirt, he looked the epitome of a successful businessman. Shelby smiled at him. He made her sister so happy, she would always cherish him for that. Would she find a love so strong one day?

"We're ready," Margot said. Her maternity dress was pure elegance—and not far different in style from the wedding gown she'd worn only a few weeks earlier for the renewal of their vows.

"Wait, we need a lucky penny," Georgia said.

"Allow me," Rand said, reaching into his trousers. He brought out a gold coin. "I've had this since I found it as a kid on the bayou. It's brought me luck over the years. Let's hope it does for you, Shelby."

"Thank you." Her eyes met those of every one. "I'm glad you're my family."

"And in a few more hours we'll add another with Patrick."

"Oh, dear," Shelby said. "I forgot to tell you about Mollie."

"Who?"

"Patrick's daughter. Mollie's four. She'll be joining the family, too."

"You're going to be a stepmother? Why didn't you say something?" Georgia asked.

Margot shook her head. "Georgia, you idiot, she's in love with Patrick. That he has a child is an extra bonus, but her mind is on him. I can understand. Let's go. I can't wait to meet her. We don't want to be late. I wouldn't expect a lot of traffic on a Saturday, but you never know."

The judge's chambers looked crowded when Shelby entered. For a moment she almost panicked. Then reason took control. She went to greet two of her co-workers—both longtime friends. She had invited them to allay any suspicions Margot might have had. Then she greeted a man and woman she didn't know, Patrick's employees. Glancing at her watch, she noted it was almost the agreed time.

Nervous, she spoke with the judge and checked the door. Where was Patrick? He hadn't changed *his* mind, had he?

Just before noon, he entered, carrying Mollie on one arm and a big bouquet of flowers in the other hand. The child looked adorable. Her hair was cut short as a pixie with a blue ribbon bow centered on the top. Her dress did make her look like a fairy princess, Shelby thought, smiling at the child with affection. She felt as proud of how sweet Mollie looked as if she were truly her mother.

Then her gaze moved to Patrick and she stood still. He looked fantastic. His charcoal gray suit and pale blue shirt fitted as though they'd been made especially for him. They emphasized his broad shoulders, his height, and the darkness of his tan. She forced in a breath and moved closer, aware of only Patrick in the gathering of friends and relatives.

''You made it,'' she said inanely, wishing she knew better how to relate to men, how to scintillate and interest.

''Thanks to Mrs. Turner across the street. These buttons are too tiny!''

Shelby's sisters immediately joined them. She introduced Georgia and was surprised when Georgia held out her arms to see Mollie lean right into them.

"I'll hold this pretty girl while the ceremony takes place. Then we'll sit together at lunch. Want to do that, Mollie?"

"Wif my bear?"

"Sure thing, sugar."

"Where is the bear, and the cap?" Shelby asked.

"Both in the car. Mollie gets to have them as soon as we leave here," Patrick said, holding out the flowers.

"These are for you. A bride needs more than a corsage."

As soon as she took them he reached out to draw her into his arms. Without another word, he kissed her long and hard.

Shelby was acutely conscious of every person in the room staring at them. She knew he was playing his role, but for a moment let herself float on the sensations that swept through her. And wished it were for real as she kissed him back.

"Dearly Beloved—" the judge began a few minutes later.

Patrick stood in front of the man and tried not to let the words remind him of another time. This marriage would be nothing like his first one. He glanced at Shelby, disconcerted to find her solemn gaze on him. Slowly he winked, pleased to note the hint of color that flooded her cheeks. Gradually she relaxed. He wished he could.

But the situation was too fraught with problems. How could he have agreed to another marriage? Hadn't the problems in the first been enough to ensure he never tried it again?

Shelby was different from Sylvia, a small voice reminded him. He'd have to remember that.

Glancing around quickly, he looked at Shelby's sisters. They didn't look alike, except for the Beaufort blue eyes. Margot had dark hair while Georgia's was a honey-blond. He liked Shelby's rich auburn color the best.

How would they all take this mock marriage when the truth was revealed?

"Do you, Patrick—"

He had to pay attention. Time enough later to figure out how he'd convinced himself this was a good idea.

CHAPTER FIVE

"I NOW pronounce you man and wife. You may kiss your bride," the judge finished.

Patrick took full advantage. Shelby's eyes widened as he pulled her into his embrace. She had a knack of always looking so surprised when he touched her or said something the slightest bit provocative. Unfortunately, the trait only had him finding more ways to surprise her and see that reaction.

Her lips were warm and soft. Whatever else, he liked kissing her. Far too much, he thought a moment later when he pulled back to the gentle laughter of their guests. Yet it seemed too brief a kiss.

Shelby's face flamed with color. Feeling a certain sense of satisfaction to have caused that reaction, Patrick grinned and turned to face the others.

"Congratulations!" someone called.

In no time their friends and family surged around to offer felicitations and hugs. Patrick endured them good-naturedly. At least for the time being he had his personal life under some control. Shelby would take care of Mollie for him and let him concentrate on business.

Playing the role of devoted husband would not be a hardship. He threaded his fingers through hers and smiled, liking the feelings he experienced around her. Except for a state of awareness he hadn't experienced since he had been a teenager.

"Welcome to the family," Georgia said as she reached up to give him a hug, Mollie between them. "We got a double bonus today, with both you and Mollie. She's a sweetheart."

Mollie beamed at her father. "This is Auntie Georgia."

"I know she is." For a moment the term threw him. Doubt rose. Was he doing the right thing for Mollie? Would she become attached to Shelby and her family? They were nice people, and without letting them know of the temporary nature of this marriage, would they become a part of their lives? Only to be missed when the marriage ended?

Maybe he should not have agreed to Shelby's request for secrecy.

Before he could think more along those lines, Bethany, one of Shelby's friends from work, brought out her camera and began to organize a series of poses of the wedding party. Then the entire group moved to one of the restaurants nearby where Shelby had made reservations.

The luncheon was perfect. The guests brought gifts which were piled on a table against the wall. Toasts were offered to the newly married couple. Georgia and Margot had arranged for a wedding cake. Mollie was enchanted with the small man and woman on top and claimed them for her own once the cake had been cut. She had her bear in tow, but had left the cap in the car.

"This is for you," Margot said, slipping an envelope to Shelby as she and Rand came over when the guests were getting ready to leave. "We didn't want to put it with the other gifts for fear you wouldn't open it until tomorrow or something.''

"What is it?''

Margot smiled broadly. "Rand and I are treating you both for a night at Le Carillon,'' she said. ''Georgia said she and her friends are moving your things to Patrick's this weekend, so we thought we'd treat tonight at the hotel. And I want to keep Mollie, if she'll come. Get me in practice.''

Shelby's mind spun. She looked at Patrick in panic. They had done nothing about Georgia's plans to move her things. Now this. What could she do without giving away the reason for their arrangement? The terms of this marriage?

Margot waited expectantly. Taking a deep breath, Shelby smiled. She hugged Margot and then Rand. "Wow, this is so great! Thank you. I didn't expect anything like this.'' Desperately she sought for a reason to decline, but none came to mind.

Patrick put his arm around Shelby and added his thanks. "We couldn't take a honeymoon just yet, but this will be a start. We appreciate it.''

The touch of his hand on her shoulder almost short-circuited Shelby's brain. She was aware of every inch of the man, of his rumbling laughter, of his muscles as he leaned forward a bit to shake Rand's hand, the warmth that radiated. How could anyone be expected to make decisions when thoughts of kisses and caresses dominated?

"We'll help you take the gifts home. If you want to open them before you go, we can then pack something for Mollie and be off,'' Margot said.

"I expect both you and Mollie could use a nap," Rand said.

"You're right. But this has been a wonderful day!"

Shelby's cheeks ached with her smile. She felt like such a fraud. But it was for a good cause, she reminded herself. Patrick would find their father. And she would make sure sweet little Mollie was able to remain with hers.

The room at Le Carillon was luxurious, as would be expected from one of New Orleans' five-star hotels. With a view of the old French Quarter and the slow-moving Mississippi River beyond, it appealed to the senses in every way. Bright blossoms filled vases around the sitting room. The thick carpet had Shelby wanting to slip off her shoes and walk barefoot. The muted colors blended with a soothing elegance.

When the bellman left, Shelby turned to look at Patrick. They were alone in this lovely suite, and had to stay until morning!

"I didn't know how to get out of it," she began.

"Not without clueing in your sister and brother-in-law," he agreed, walking around examining the furnishings. Stopping by the window, he looked at the view.

"And Georgia, she meant well, too."

"You are lucky to have such a close family. They're happy for you and want to share that happiness."

"I know. I feel like such a fraud."

Patrick turned around, leaned against the glass, his hands in the pockets of his trousers. "Why?"

"They think this is real."

"The marriage is real."

She looked surprised. "Yes, it is, isn't it? But I mean they think we are in love and will stay together forever. All the people at the wedding thought it was real. What do we do with all the wedding presents?"

"Write thank-you notes?"

Shelby frowned and moved to sink down on the sofa. "We got them under false pretenses."

Patrick shook his head. "Shelby, we got married. We will stay married at least for several months. The people we invited today were happy to share in what they thought was a special day for us. Let them have the fun of giving gifts. If your sensibilities won't allow it, when we split, you can return them."

She let Patrick's words wash through her. Idly tracing the pattern on the sofa fabric, she admitted she was trying to find something to talk about. She was more concerned about spending the night in this hotel suite alone with Patrick. Would he expect more from her than she could give?

What would they talk about? It was hours until morning. Even if they went out to dinner and a movie or something, she wasn't sure she could last until time to leave tomorrow.

If it had been someone else, maybe. But she was growing more and more interested in the man who had just become her husband. He was totally different from anyone she knew. Not that she knew him that well.

Venturing a glance in his direction, she was startled to find him staring at her.

"What?"

"Just thinking. Want to change into something more comfortable? I do."

She nodded, wondering with a touch of trepidation if he expected them to change together in the bedroom.

He pushed away and went toward the bedroom door. "I'll change, then leave it to you." Pausing at the doorway, he looked over his shoulder. "You look lovely in your suit and hat. I'm glad your friend took those pictures."

Shelby felt the breath leave her at that statement. The door closed and she leaned back on the sofa, feeling confused and flustered. He was glad for the pictures? She thought he'd endured the process just to further their charade.

Smiling, she remembered Bethany's insistence on all the different poses: she and Patrick, she, Patrick and Mollie, pictures with the judge, with her sisters, and several group shots with everyone. For a second, Shelby wistfully wished it had been a real wedding. One meant to last.

Sighing, she rose and crossed to the window, her ears attuned toward the bedroom. When Patrick finished changing, she would take off her wedding finery and put on something more suitable.

Maybe they could go for a walk or something. She felt restless and unsettled, and far too fascinated with the man in the next room.

An hour later they strolled along the River. Shelby sought for something to talk about, but felt as tongue-tied as a teenager on a first date. She cleared her throat.

"Did you get a chance to talk to Edith Strong yet?" she asked.

He shook his head. "No, I tried calling, but the nursing home discouraged that. I thought we could ride up one day and see her. She knows you and will be more forthcoming, I'm sure, if you're there.''

"Oh. Okay."

Silence. The hot Louisiana sun beat down on them. The only cooling grace was the slight breeze blowing from the water.

Patrick reached for her arm, turning her toward a vacant bench in the shade of an old oak.

"Let's sit and talk."

Shelby nodded, nerves stretched taut. "About what?"

Patrick waited until they sat, then looked out across the water. "About us and this marriage."

She cleared her throat. "Okay." Her heart thrummed in her chest, her hands grew damp and she wiped them surreptitiously on her skirt.

"I'll be blunt. I'm attracted to you, Shelby. You must have recognized that. I didn't expect it and didn't want it, but there it is."

"That's blunt," she blurted out, her eyes wide as she stared at Patrick. What did he want her to say?

He grimaced slightly, then gave her a half smile. "Yeah, well, that's the best way, I think. The thing is, I didn't plan to marry again. My relationship with Sylvia wasn't the best recommendation for a second try."

"I remember you didn't exactly leap at the chance to marry when I first brought it up."

"But I'm glad you did. And I appreciate what you're planning to do for Mollie. And me. I don't know how I could have managed without this arrangement. And the last thing I wanted was to send her away. So maybe the next to last thing I wanted was to get involved again.''

''Involved?''

He reached out to trace a finger along her cheek, as if fascinated by the texture of her skin.

''You are so soft,'' he said slowly.

Heat rushed through Shelby at his touch. Heat and a yearning that grew stronger each time she was with Patrick.

''What is it you want, Patrick?''

''I want you, Shelby O'Shaunnessy.''

The world spun. Shelby gripped the edge of the bench to keep from flying off. Had she heard him correctly?

''I know we planned on a platonic relationship. And I'll stick with that, if you like. But I don't think this attraction is all one-sided and I wanted you to know where I stand.'' He dropped his hand and turned, arms crossed, to gaze at the river.

''I don't know quite what to say,'' she said a few second later. The silence seemed to reverberate.

''You don't have to say anything unless you want to agree to an affair while we're married.''

She smiled. ''An affair while we are married, that sounds weird.''

He looked at her and shrugged. ''Temporary like this marriage. What would you call it?''

She swallowed. He was serious. *He wanted her!* Oh wow!

''We don't even know each other very well.''

''So we did it backwards, got married, then learned about each other. What do you want to know?''

''Everything.'' Shelby surprised herself with the intensity of her curiosity. She wanted to learn every scrap of information she could about Patrick.

"Where you were born, grew up. Where your parents are now. What you were like as a little boy. What made you become a private investigator."

He stretched out his feet and settled on the bench. "Short version: born here in New Orleans. I have two brothers, neither of whom live here now. My folks are both dead, no grandparents living, but they were all around when I was a kid. The only other relatives Mollie has are her mother's parents in Atlanta. I went to school at Tulane, got a law degree, decided I liked investigating more than prosecuting or defending, so switched from practicing law to detective work." He arched an eyebrow as his gaze met hers. "Anything more?"

"That's short, all right."

"So tell me your life story."

"In twenty-five words or less?"

"In as many words as you need."

"What don't you already know from your investigation of my background?"

"Whether you've ever been in love. Why you aren't married. Why you moved to New Orleans right after high school."

"I thought I was in love once—in high school. I am married now—to you. And I left Natchez as soon as I could to escape my domineering grandmother."

"And no current boyfriend?"

She shook her head.

Patrick was silent for a long moment. "Have you ever had an affair before?"

Shelby shook her head again.

He groaned softly and leaned back on the bench. "So that wide-eyed innocent act isn't really an act at all?"

"What wide-eyed innocent act?"

"Never mind. I've put my cards on the table. You let me know if you want to pick them up."

"Patrick, I don't think having an affair is such a good idea. This is just a temporary arrangement while you locate my father. We don't want to complicate things." Shelby tried for a calm rational argument, but her heart was still racing out of control and a major part of her wanted to throw herself into his arms and agree to any terms he wanted.

But where would that leave her when it came time to end their marriage? She was already fascinated by the man. If there was any physical intimacy between them would she endanger her heart as well?

He rose. "If you change your mind, you let me know. Come on, I want to walk."

The rest of the afternoon spun by. Shelby was worried at first that Patrick would push her to comply with his outrageous suggestion. But he never even hinted. They were simply two people thrown together by circumstances who had to spend time together. He questioned her about her father, trying to gather as much information as she could provide.

Then they spoke of Mollie, of the renovations in the downtown area, and of the chances of the Saints for next year's Super Bowl.

When they returned to their suite after dinner, Patrick located the television and turned it on.

"The sofa folds out into a bed, I'll take that," he said as he kicked off his shoes.

Shelby was touched. Had he seen how nervous she was when they returned? "Thank you. I think I'll go to bed now, if you don't mind. It's been a long day." And she hadn't slept all that well the night before.

"Let me get my suitcase."

Ten minutes later Shelby slipped beneath the cool sheets and turned off the light. She could hear the low murmur of the television. For a moment she wondered if she was doing right to resist his offer of an affair. They were married. And she hadn't met anyone in her life she admired as much as Patrick. Normally shy and uncertain, she gradually grew more comfortable in his company. Who knew if she'd ever find a man to fall in love with and marry. Maybe she should take Patrick up on his offer.

Patrick was already up and dressed and raring to go when Shelby came out of the bedroom the next morning.

"I miss Mollie," he said with a sheepish grin. "This is only the second night we've been apart since she came to live with me last year. I had a trip I couldn't avoid when I had one of the housekeepers to watch her."

"Don't you want to eat, first?" Shelby asked, touched at his revelation.

Patrick glanced at his watch, and nodded. "It is a bit early. We don't want Margot to think we didn't enjoy the stay."

"Thank you for going along with all that. We are counting on her having a fine healthy baby. And I sure don't want to add any worry at this stage. She's nervous enough as it is."

"Chances should be good that the baby will be fine."

"So her doctor says."

"Tell me more about Georgia. Mollie sure took to her yesterday."

Shelby nodded, feeling just a hint of the jealousy that had hit her yesterday. She wanted Mollie to like her, but they had never hit it off as well as the instant rapport between Georgia and the little girl.

They ordered breakfast and Shelby talked about her sisters, and gave Patrick a glimpse into her life at her grandmother's. He added comments comparing his childhood with hers and she gleaned a broader perspective of his own background.

When they picked up Mollie, she wore her blue ribbon instead of the baseball cap, and carried her dressed-up teddy bear. She gave Margot and Rand huge hugs and waved all the way down the street as they headed for Patrick's house. On the ride, Mollie spoke almost nonstop about staying with Auntie Margot and Unca Rand. Shelby smiled at her chatter, hoping Mollie would soon feel as comfortable with her as she had with her sisters.

When they arrived home, Patrick carried the two small overnight cases into his bedroom. Shelby followed, carrying her wedding outfit. Standing near the bed, he surveyed the room. Except for a few items on the dresser, it didn't look different from when he left. But striding to the closet and opening the door, he saw dresses and blouses hanging side by side with his own suits. Colorful high heels competed for floor space with his own dark shoes.

"I'll move everything into the other room," Shelby

said, coming to stand beside him. "If you and Mollie want to play out back as she suggested, I can do it now."

He reached out a finger and tilted her chin. Brushing his lips across hers, he then looked into her eyes.

"Remember what I said, you just give the word."

Flustered, Shelby nodded, longing to throw caution to the wind and at least *consider* his amazing suggestion. With dazed eyes, she watched him stride from the room and call Mollie.

Soon the sound of childish laugher came in through the open window. Shelby detoured by the window, her arms full of dresses, to look out. Patrick was playing ball with Mollie. He'd gently lob the big ball toward the little girl's outstretched hands. The ball would actually bounce against one palm or the other, then fall to the grass. Laughing, she'd race to pick it up and throw it back to her father. Once in a while, Patrick managed to run fast enough to catch an erratic toss.

Both of them appeared to be having a wonderful time.

Wistfully Shelby watched for long moments. Mollie was one lucky little girl. She would have wonderful memories growing up. Once again the sense of rightness filled her. If nothing else, Shelby was glad she had made this possible.

But she felt oddly left out. Patrick had not included her. Sighing softly, she carried her dresses to her room.

Monday morning Patrick left early. Mollie was still eating breakfast. Shelby had dressed for work before preparing the meal, so she was ready. As soon as Mollie was finished, they'd leave for the office and Mollie's new day care center.

"Hurry up, Mollie. We need to leave soon," Shelby said as the child dawdled over her milk.

"Don't gots to," Mollie mumbled. She wore her baseball hat today, and her teddy bear waited on the floor beside her chair.

"Don't have to. Don't say got, say have." Shelby murmured, checking the time again. She planned to drive to work rather than subject Mollie to the bus, but wasn't sure how heavy the traffic would be from Patrick's house. She wanted to leave plenty of time to take Mollie to the day care and still make it on time to her desk.

"Are you finished with your milk?"

"No." She fiddled with the glass.

"Mollie, we have to go."

Mollie's lower lip pushed out and she glared at Shelby. "Don't gots to."

"Yes, you do have to. You are going to a new day care today. We need to be there on time. Come on."

"NO!" Mollie scooted off her chair, snatched up her bear and ran for her room.

Nonplused, Shelby stared after her for a long moment. Patrick had said she was a handful sometimes. Had she or her sisters ever behaved like that with their grandmother? Somehow she doubted it.

She put everything in the car and went to get Mollie. Maybe she'd call Georgia later and ask for pointers.

"Come on, Mollie. Time to go."

"Don't gots to," Mollie stated from her position on her bed. She had her back to the door.

Shelby crossed the room and knelt beside the bed,

trying to catch Mollie's eye. "I'll tell you what. If you come now like a good girl, we'll stop at the park on the way home. How about that?"

Warily Mollie studied Shelby. After a long moment, she nodded and crawled to the edge of the bed. "Okay. I can go on the swing?"

"Yes." Relieved they were heading out, Shelby ignored the bribery aspect, though her own words echoed in her mind. Right now she was looking for whatever worked. Once she and Mollie got to know each other, she'd know better how to deal with the child. And there was no reason Patrick should ever find out about today's bribe.

Patrick checked out the front window for the eighteenth time in the last half hour. Where were they? He knew Shelby normally left work at five. Had she had to work late? Couldn't she have called? What if they had been in a traffic accident? It didn't take ninety minutes to drive from her office building to the house.

He paced the living room, checking his watch again. He'd already called her office, but reached only a recording announcing the office hours. He didn't dare call Margot, Shelby's admonitions were too strong. Georgia would be at work. He remembered her talking about her days off and how she had switched with others to get the weekend off.

Where were they?

A car turned into the driveway. Rushing to the door, he flung it wide open and stepped outside. Shelby released Mollie from the seat belt in back, leaning in through the open door. The relief to see them both safe mingled with the attraction he felt for his new wife. He wanted to yell at her for putting him through this worry, then snatch her close and kiss her breathless.

Instead, he clenched his fists and waited with what patience he could muster as they came toward him.

Mollie ran ahead, her teddy bear bumping against her leg.

"Hi Daddy. I went on the swings. I went really high." She flung herself into his arms when he stooped to her level. Lifting her, he hugged her close.

"Where have you two been?" he demanded when Shelby drew closer.

"We stopped at the park." She looked at him closely. "Is something wrong?"

"You scare the h—" he glanced at his daughter. "You scared me when you weren't home when I arrived. I thought you left work at five."

"I did. Mollie and I stopped at the park." She bit her lip as a look of contrition crossed her face. "I'm sorry, Patrick, I didn't even think you might be home or worried. I'm not used to living with anyone."

He couldn't help himself. Reaching for her with his free hand, he drew her close enough to kiss. Just the touch of her lips against his sent his temperature soaring. He wanted her and wondered if she'd given any thought to his proposal.

"You do now! Maybe I overreacted, but I was worried when you both weren't home where I expected you to be," he said, releasing her and turning toward the open door.

"I'll call next time," she said breathlessly.

Patrick smiled. At least he got the kissing part right. But if he weren't holding Mollie in one arm, he would have done a lot more of that.

"I have a cell phone, I'll give you the number. Maybe we should get you one, in case you have trouble when in the car or something."

"Okay. Sorry you were worried. We were fine, weren't we, Mollie?"

The little girl nodded and smiled at her father. "I went high on the swing."

"You did. Good for you. What else did you do at the park?"

"Tell your Daddy all we did, Mollie. I'm going to change and then start dinner."

Patrick listened with half an ear to Mollie's excited chatter as he watched Shelby take the stairs to the second story. He hadn't only been worried about Mollie, but about Shelby as well. Which didn't make sense. She'd been right on Saturday, they hardly knew each other.

So why did the thought of her in trouble bring out all the protective instincts he possessed?

CHAPTER SIX

SHELBY changed, feeling odd. It had been a long time since anyone had worried about where she was. There was obviously more to this marriage than she originally anticipated. But it felt nice. At first she thought Patrick had been concerned solely about Mollie. Not so. He'd been worried about her as well.

When she went to the kitchen, she saw the two of them in the backyard again. The weather had cooled and it probably felt good to play outside. And Mollie sure had enough energy for it. If Patrick ran some more of it off, the child would sleep well tonight.

As Shelby prepared a light supper, she tried not to dwell on the kiss Patrick had bestowed when she arrived home tonight. But it was impossible. It had been hard and quick. She wondered what it meant. Just relief, probably, from the worry that he'd experienced when they had not arrived when expected. Or had there been more in it? Had she felt a trace of possession?

When dinner was ready, she went to the door that led to the yard. For a second she watched Patrick and Mollie play. Shelby longed to run out and join them, but they looked so self-contained she felt like an outsider. Would they want her to join them?

"Dinner is ready," she called.

Patrick looked up and waved, scooping up his daughter and jogging toward Shelby.

"We're starving, right Mollie?"

The little girl laughed as she clung to her father and nodded. "Starving!"

"Well then it's a good thing I made lots of dinner, isn't it?" Shelby said as they swept past her and headed to the downstairs bathroom to wash up.

For the first time in years, Shelby felt part of a family as the three of them sat at the table to eat. Mollie told her father all about her first day at the day care and then about their adventure in the park. Patrick asked lots of questions and paid close attention to every word.

His gaze met Shelby's on more than one occasion. He'd smile and wink, as if including her. She hadn't enjoyed a meal so much since she'd been a little girl having supper with just her two sisters.

"I've brought a ton of work home. The records and billing are a mess. After Mollie is in bed, I'll take you up on your offer of some help, if you're not too tired," he said as they finished eating.

Shelby nodded, feeling even more included. "That will be fine, I don't feel tired at all." Full of energy and excited described how she felt.

Shelby loved organizing things. She had already re-arranged a few items in the kitchen to make it a more efficient work space. While Patrick was bathing Mollie, she plunged into the stack of papers he'd shown her. Everything was mixed up and she had to skim each sheet to get an idea of what it was. But soon she had several distinct piles of reports, billing information, correspondence and legal regulations.

"Shelby?" Patrick called from upstairs.

"Yes?"

"Can you come tell Mollie good-night?"

Jumping up, she hurried to the stairs, a warm glow

beginning to spread through her. She had told Mollie good-night when she went up for her bath, but to be requested to come when she was tucked in bed was definite progress.

She entered Mollie's room and smiled at the little girl all tucked up in her bed.

"Good night, sweetie. I hope you sleep well."

"Kissy?" Mollie said, holding up her arms.

Shelby's heart melted. She crossed the room and drew the child close, relishing her fresh scent, the soft sweetness she cuddled in her arms. Kissing her cheek she laid her back down and tucked her teddy bear near her.

"Tomorrow we'll go to day care again. I'm glad you liked it."

"And have eggs for breakfast?"

"Sure, eggs for breakfast. Nighty-night."

Patrick had already left the room by the time Shelby rose. She switched off the light, but left the door ajar as she went in search of him. Wanting to dance down the hall at the change in Mollie's attitude, she nevertheless maintained a dignified walk. Her grandmother had always believed any bursts of enthusiasm or wild rejoicing were unladylike. And it was hard sometimes to let go of old taboos.

Patrick lounged on the sofa with one of the stacks of papers on his lap. He lay down the sheet he'd been reading when Shelby entered.

"All set?"

"I think she'll be asleep in seconds. That was nice."

"What?"

"That she wanted me to kiss her good-night."

He shrugged and picked up the paper again. "She is

a bit cautious around strangers, but she'll warm up to you.''

"She took to Georgia immediately," Shelby said without thinking.

He raised an eyebrow. "Jealous?"

Smiling sheepishly, she nodded. "I guess I am. Dumb, huh?"

His gaze was serious. "I don't think so. You want her to like you and she's been difficult. Of course Auntie Georgia's relationship will be different. And Georgia has a totally different personality from you."

"More fun."

"Certainly more lighthearted. Lighten up a bit, Shelby. You're too young to be so serious."

"I've always been serious."

"So kick over the traces and try something different."

"I'll take your advice under advisement."

Patrick laughed. "Do as you like. I don't want you to change too much, you're all right as you are." He began reading again.

Shelby sank on a nearby chair, her knees feeling decidedly weak. As compliments went, it sure hadn't been spectacular, but to her, it sounded wonderful.

For a long time there was silence in the room as they each worked. Once Shelby had sorted all the papers, she took a pile and put it in chronological order. The work was not difficult, basic record retention. But from the stack of papers, she knew Patrick's business was behind in billings, and in responding to some of his clients. He needed to catch up soon or impact the bottom line.

Shelby said good-night sometime later. Patrick was

still working his way through a stack of papers, jotting notes in the margins, or attaching sheets with his scribble on it.

As she prepared for bed, she again thought of his wild proposal on Saturday. What would it be like to make love with Patrick? To give in to the fantasies that filled her nights? She didn't have any experience with that. She was twenty-five years old. Was there someone out there for her, or was she destined to remain alone once this marriage ended? She had never thought much about it before. Now she thought about it all the time. Especially since Patrick told her he wanted her.

The kisses they shared would only be the beginning. And she knew she could scarcely think after one. What would it be like to move on?

Hurriedly brushing her teeth, she left the bathroom in case Patrick was waiting to use it before bed. She dashed down the hall to the safety of her own room. But the closed door did not shut off the images that danced in her mind. Climbing into bed, she shut her eyes, and relived every kiss the man had given her. It didn't soothe her for sleep.

Patrick threw down his pen and picked up the phone to call Shelby late Tuesday morning. He just wanted to hear her voice.

"Is something wrong?" she asked when he identified himself.

"No. I just wanted to let you know that thanks to you, the temp is able to do more than just answer the phone today. She's doing several reports and I'll be able to issue invoices once the clients receive their reports."

"Good. You know, if you had a computer at home, we could do some of that work in the evenings, to get you caught up even faster."

He was surprised. Sylvia never offered any help. She'd resented his work and time he spent on the job.

"I suppose I could bring one home from the office for a while," he said slowly.

"At least until you get your billing caught up. We can work after Mollie is in bed each night."

"How did Mollie do this morning?"

"Fine. At least today she didn't give me her famous 'don't gots to' routine."

Patrick laughed. "Bad habit, huh?"

"Patrick," Shelby's tone turned mocking. "You have to teach her proper manners so she can take her rightful place in society."

He laughed again. He seemed to do that a lot around Shelby. "Was that your grandmother's influence?"

"Yes. And it sounds funny now, but it didn't when I was growing up. You're lucky I didn't buy into all her lecturing or Mollie would be whisked off to finishing school before you knew it."

"You wouldn't do that to such a little girl." He knew Shelby's heart was too soft.

"No, I wouldn't. I think it's wonderful she has such a great dad. I'm glad you let me help so you could keep her with you."

Patrick studied the clouds in the distance through the window. "Is that the only reason you're glad about our marriage?" He didn't know why he wanted to push the issue, but he wanted something more.

"Of course not. You're going to find my father, aren't you?"

The disappointment surprised him. Those were the terms of the marriage. Even when he'd told her he wanted a more physical relationship, she hadn't agreed.

"Yeah. I'll bring a computer home tonight and we can start catching up on getting some money."

"I'm happy to help," she said diffidently.

"You planning to get straight home today?"

"Yes. We don't need to stop at the park. I'll tell Mollie you called when I see her at lunch."

"You don't have to spend your lunch hour with her every day," Patrick said.

"I know, and there will be days when I won't. But that's one of the nice features of having the day care in the building, parents can spend time with their children during the day. It's a good way for us to get to know each other."

He thought of her jealousy of Georgia and knew she wanted the extra time to try to establish the same kind of rapport.

"Give her a kiss for me and I'll see you both tonight."

Patrick hung up but didn't move for a long time. Shelby was proving to be unexpected in more ways than one. Initially he thought she proposed this marriage just to get information on her father. But her attempts to draw closer to Mollie and her offers to help him were surprising. Sylvia would never have done such a thing.

In fact, Sylvia had complained long and hard about the extra hours and then complained about the lack of money. She liked to play and had never been content with what he provided. She had been a good mother, but wanted things on her terms.

Shelby was quite different, shy and quiet, but generous. And so beautiful it hurt to look at her and not draw her into his arms.

By Friday, they were well entrenched in a definite pattern. Patrick called each day just before lunch. He never stayed on the phone long, but made sure he checked on Mollie and Shelby.

In the evenings, once Mollie was in bed, they worked on the computer he set up. The billing was brought up to date. Shelby had several suggestions on work flow that Patrick tried and discovered they streamlined things a great deal. He began telling her about some of his cases and she related what she and Mollie did at lunchtime, or the frustrations of dealing with one of the partners in the firm.

But in other areas, they made no progress, in Patrick's opinion. He made it a point to kiss Shelby when she arrived home each night, hoping she'd give some indication that she'd like to change the status quo. She returned his kisses, but then every night she seemed to deliberately wait until he was engrossed in something before slipping off to bed.

He was growing more and more frustrated. He'd put his cards on the table, and had to admit he had expected her to do something about his suggestion. Instead, she seemed to be ignoring the situation entirely. He wondered how much longer he'd let her set the pace. She was driving him crazy!

He knew she felt the attraction between them. She'd respond to his kisses like a kid in a candy shop. Then pull back, wide-eyed and breathless. If Mollie wasn't always present, he'd demand another kiss and see where it led.

Finishing up early on Friday, Patrick was just about ready to leave when the phone rang. He'd wanted to get a jump on the traffic, expecting the holiday weekend to clog the roadways.

"Patrick, it's Shelby."

"What's wrong?" He could hear the tension in her voice.

"Nothing major, but my car won't start. I was expecting to leave a little early and already have Mollie. When I tried to start the engine, it wouldn't. It makes a funny whirring sound."

"I'll be there in a few minutes."

"I'm parked in the lot near the building. I'll watch for you."

Patrick grabbed the folder he had for the Sam Williams search and headed out. Tomorrow he planned to drive to Natchez to interview Edith Strong. Shelby and Mollie were going with him. If they left early enough, they'd be in Natchez by lunch. After they talked with Mrs. Strong, he'd like to take a swing by the house, Beaufort Hall, that Shelby had mentioned briefly. To see where Shelby had grown up, and maybe find out why she had no attachment to the place.

But first, he had to go get his family.

An hour later Patrick slammed down the hood of the car and wiped his hands on a cloth he'd had in his trunk.

"Can't fix it, babe. We'll have to have it towed to a garage." With the long weekend for Independence Day, it would be sometime next week before a garage would be able to fix it.

"Rats. It's been making a funny noise for a few weeks, but I thought it would go away," Shelby said in disgust.

He looked at her. "Go away? Usually when things are making a funny noise, it's a symptom something is wrong."

"It made a funny noise a few years ago and then it went away."

"Get in the car, Shelby. I'll call the garage when we get home."

Shelby grabbed her purse and helped Mollie from the front seat of her car. "We're riding in Daddy's car tonight, punkin."

"Even though it doesn't look like much, it runs," Patrick said as he opened the door for Shelby.

She frowned and looked at the door. "It didn't squeak."

Slowly Patrick smiled at her. "I told you I'd oil it."

Shelby's pulse rate increased at the sight of that devastating smile. Feeling confused she slid into the car and waited while he closed the door. The silent door. When Patrick opened his own, Mollie scrambled into the backseat and waited while her father buckled the seat belt.

"Thank you," Shelby said softly, touched he'd made a change for her.

Patrick nodded and slid behind the wheel. "You only have to tell me what you want, Shelby, and I'll do my best to see you get it. And I always do what I say I will."

Tell him what she wanted? Like more kisses? she almost asked. Was there some way she could let him know that she was receptive to his suggestion they take this marriage a bit farther?

Of course, he was probably looking for a declaration of intent. And she was not sure she could give voice to the churning emotions that confused her. Each time he kissed her, she wanted it to go on forever. If Patrick hadn't changed his mind, she had to find a way to let him know she had changed hers!

Turning, her eye caught the folder on the middle of the seat. The label was clear. It was the one for her father. Feeling like a deflated balloon, she sighed and looked out the front window. She had better remember exactly why she and Patrick had agreed to this marriage. He might want a fling, an affair, but nothing had been said about forever. And Shelby had a feeling she was a forever kind of person.

When Shelby came down for breakfast the next morning, Mollie and her father were already eating cereal for breakfast.

"Going for a ride," Mollie said proudly.

"I know that, sweetheart. We're going to the town where I used to live." Shelby smiled at the child, and then Patrick, her breath catching when she saw him. After a week of sharing a house, she should be used to the reaction. But it always caught her by surprise. Trying to get control of her wayward thoughts, she popped some bread in the toaster.

He looked wonderful in the light blue shirt and faded jeans—like a family man ready for a casual outing with his wife and child.

She wondered if Mrs. Strong would be able to provide any helpful information that would speed his investigation.

"Do you have sunscreen?" Patrick asked when Shelby sat at the table with her toast and tea a few minutes later.

"Yes, why?"

"We'll all need it today. I'm renting a convertible for the trip."

Shelby looked at him. "Why?"

"Why not? Don't you think that would be fun? It's a beautiful day, not as hot as it was earlier in the week, and I think it would be more fun to drive with the top down and really be able to see things. Fun for Mollie, too."

"I think it would be fantastic! I've always wanted to ride in one."

"Then today is your lucky day!"

Patrick and Mollie left right after breakfast to see about renting the car. Shelby straightened up while she waited. Hurriedly dusting and vacuuming the main floor, she was surprised at the sense of belonging. Granted, Georgia and her friends had skillfully mingled her furnishings with Patrick's so she felt a bit more at home. But this was something more.

As she picked up Mollie's toys, she felt a sense of connection. Was this what being part of a close family was like? She liked it.

Glancing at her watch, she wondered if she had time to start a load of laundry. It must have piled up over the week and she needed to get a start if she wanted everything done before the next work week started.

Gathering Mollie's clothes, Shelby then headed for Patrick's room. She had not been in it since she moved her things out last Sunday. Pausing in the doorway, she caught her breath. His scent filled her senses. Slowly she studied the room, seeing Patrick's stamp everywhere, from the tumble of keys and change on his dresser, to the carelessly tossed socks and jeans near, but not quite in, the hamper. His bed was rumpled. Didn't he make it each morning?

They all shared the hall bathroom, and he was pretty neat there, hanging up his towel and clearing away his shaving things. But he obviously felt free to do what he pleased in his own room.

Which was as it should be, Shelby thought as she gathered the clothes.

Patrick and Mollie arrived in a bright red convertible a few minutes later. Mollie called Shelby from the car, standing up in the front seat.

"Come and see!" she squealed when Shelby appeared at the front door.

Jumping up and down she raised her hands over her head. "No roof, Shelby, no roof!"

"Easy, squirt. Don't go tumbling out." Patrick reached for her shirt, to keep her from losing her balance.

"I see—no roof." Shelby laughed at the child's enthusiasm.

She was a lucky little girl to have such an indulgent father. Shelby's grandmother would never have tolerated such behavior. Yet why shouldn't a child share her exuberance?

"Ready?" Patrick called.

"Just a second." Shelby closed up and hurried down the sidewalk to the dashing car.

"Jump over the side, Shelby," Mollie instructed.

"I think I better open the door first, honey."

"Daddy dropped me over the side and jumped in that way."

Eyeing Patrick's wide grin, Shelby laughed in sheer happiness. "I just bet he did. This time, though, I better get in the normal way."

"Chicken," Patrick said, teasing her.

"I beg your pardon."

"Live a little. Slide in over the side. Why have a convertible if you can't be bold?"

Bold? He could write the book, she thought, biting her lip in indecision. Scenes from movies flashed through her mind, hands on the side, jumping in.

"Just plant that luscious bottom on the side and lean back. We'll catch you," Patrick instructed, laughing at her.

"We'll catch you, Shelby. Do it!" Mollie shouted.

Tossing her purse into the backseat, Shelby did just that. Tumbling into the seat amidst laughter, she felt exhilarated and free. Patrick and Mollie were squished when she lost her balance, legs still over the side of the door, and fell sprawled almost the length of the seat. But no one minded.

Straightening, Shelby giggled, wanting to throw her arms around Patrick and thank him for all the ways he was changing her life. She cherished the hours she spent with him.

"Good idea, huh?" Patrick asked as he settled Mollie between them, fastening her seat belt.

"Great idea. Is this how you do all your investigations?" Shelby asked as she fastened her own belt. For the first time she felt like a different woman, one who was interesting and exciting—no longer quiet and shy.

"Not usually. But then this isn't a normal investigation."

"True. I'm ready."

"Then we're off."

The ride passed swiftly. Patrick began with telling Mollie stories. When he ran out, they all sang songs. Shelby was amazed at the lyrics she remembered from when she'd been a child. The morning was over almost before they knew it.

"Lunch and then the nursing home. I can drop you and Mollie somewhere if you like. There must be a park around somewhere," Patrick said as he entered the city limits for Natchez.

"I want to go to see Mrs. Strong. And she'd love to see Mollie. She's not ill, she just can't do everything for herself anymore. She's confined to a wheelchair, but I know she'd love to see a little girl running around. And I want to hear what she has to say. Margot and Rand spoke with her before. I only met her when they renewed their vows."

"Then lead on. Where's the best place to eat in this town?"

They met with Edith Strong on the terrace of the retirement home in the early afternoon. As Shelby predicted, she was delighted to have them visit. When Mollie expressed curiosity about her wheelchair, she invited her into her lap and gave her a ride around the terrace.

"Another vehicle with no roof," Patrick said softly to Shelby as they watched the two enjoying themselves.

"I told you Mrs. Strong would like to see Mollie. And from the look on the faces of some of the other residents, I bet that all are delighted to have her here."

A few minutes later, Patrick began his questions. Shelby was surprised at all Mrs. Strong remembered, and how much she knew about her family.

At one point, the older woman looked at her as if picking up on that surprise. "Your grandmother and I were best friends before she interfered in your mother's life. I disapproved and our friendship cooled. But there's no truth to the rumor that elderly people forget things. I'm as sharp as I ever was. As was Harriet, until the end, right?"

Shelby nodded, intrigued by the glimpses of her own life when she was a baby. Margot had said their father had loved their mother, but it seemed more real when Edith Strong talked about it.

The old sense of loss rose when she heard again how her grandmother had tried to manipulate her daughter's life in such a cruel fashion. Had Harriet Beaufort not interfered, Shelby's life would have been vastly different.

As they walked back to the car an hour later, Shelby was hit by the renewed strength of desire to locate to her father. To find out what he'd done with his life all these years. To discover if he was in need, or had moved on and made a new life for himself.

Patrick lifted Mollie over the side of the red car and set her on the seat, then opened the door for Shelby.

"You okay, babe?"

She nodded. "I will be once you find my father. It's so sad, isn't it. They were so in love and to be separated like that. You know, my sisters and I have a theory that our mother got sick and just gave up. I wonder what would have happened if she hadn't died when she did. Do you think she would have gone looking for him?"

"Yes."

She stared at him hopefully. "Really?"

"Sure. You had to get your determination and perseverance from someone, probably your mother. If she had lived, I bet she would have discovered the deception your grandmother initiated and tracked down Sam to tell him everything."

Shelby smiled, the ache in her heart easing a bit. "Thanks, Patrick. I don't know if you mean it or not, but it's nice to hear."

He placed a finger beneath her chin and raised her face, lowering his until Shelby could feel the puff of his breath against her cheeks. "Honey, I always mean what I say. You remember that!"

Nodding, Shelby couldn't move. Mesmerized by the hot look in his eyes, she knew he was also referring to his blunt statement on the riverbank last weekend. Heat seeped into her, hotter than that from the sun. Why was it just being around this man was enough to melt any common sense she possessed?

"I'll find your father for you Shelby," Patrick said softly. "And if you keep looking at me like that, I'll move it to the number one priority at the agency."

He brushed his lips across hers and then straightened.

"Wanna go for a ride!" Mollie said impatiently.

"Get in, Shelby, and show us the old family homestead."

"You want to see Beaufort Hall?" she asked in surprise.

"Sure do. You tell us how to get there."

Shelby climbed into the car and watched as Patrick went around to the driver's side, puzzled by his request. "Why? Do you think you can find some clue my father left, like an old letter in the crack of a tree?"

He grinned as he made sure Mollie was fastened in securely. "Nope, just want to see where you were raised." His gaze met hers. "Any problem with that?"

Secretly pleased, Shelby shook her head. She hadn't missed Beaufort Hall a single day since she left. But if Patrick wanted to see it, she didn't mind.

The place had an air of desertion surrounding it, she noted, as he drove down the long driveway. The trees on either side were in full leaf, the Spanish moss heavy. There were dead leaves on the verandah, and a branch or two that had obviously fallen during a recent rainstorm. No one had lived in the house since they'd put it up for sale.

Taking her keys, Shelby let them into the old mansion. It smelled musty and stale. The place had been listed for sale for a couple of months, but Margot said there'd been little interest.

"No wonder you don't like my car, if this is where you were raised," Patrick said slowly, taking in the crystal chandelier, the fine furnishings and costly paintings.

Shelby turned swiftly and crossed the entry to stand deliberately in front of him. "I might have judged your car hastily, Patrick. Don't make the same mistake about this house. It was a shrine for Harriet Beaufort, but not a place to call home by her granddaughters."

He put his big hands on her shoulders and drew her closer.

"Let's shock your grandmother's ghost," he said whimsically.

CHAPTER SEVEN

SHELBY felt a shiver of anticipation. She took a deep breath. "What did you have in mind?" She didn't trust that gleam in Patrick's eye.

He smiled and shrugged, his hands tightening slightly on her shoulders. "What would shock her the most, dancing barefoot in the entry, playing tag on the ground floor, or sliding down the bannister?"

Shelby laughed, trying to ignore the twinge of disappointment at his words. What had she expected him to say?

"All of the above! And I especially wished to slide down the bannister when I was a child," she confided.

"Can we go?" Mollie asked.

Patrick released his hold as the adults looked at her.

"Go where?" Patrick asked.

"Home."

"In a bit. We want to see Shelby's house."

Mollie's eyes widened. "This is Shelby's house?"

"It used to be, when I was a little girl like you," Shelby said. "Want to see my bedroom?"

"You gots toys?"

"Have, not gots. There aren't any toys left. We are trying to sell the house and all the personal things have been taken away. But you can see my bed and where I used to play. And I'll show you Auntie Georgia's and Auntie Margot's rooms, too."

"'Kay."

"Come on, then." Shelby reached out her hand and was pleased when Mollie trustingly placed hers in it. They climbed the long stairway to the spacious second story. Walking down the hall toward her old bedroom, Shelby was assailed with memories. Many happy ones of her and her sisters running between their rooms, telling secrets and laughing. But the echo of their grandmother's stern voice sounded. She had never evidenced any joy and seemed determined to squelch any signs in her granddaughters as well.

"This is it." Shelby stepped inside and glanced around. It was a lovely room. The windows were tall, the furniture top quality. But it looked cold and lonely.

Mollie raced to the window and gazed outside, then walked around, touching things until she came to the canopy bed. Looking at the canopy, she smiled.

"Can I get up?" she asked.

Shelby crossed to lift the child into the bed. Mollie promptly lay back and eyed the lacy confection above her head. "Like a little house," she said.

"I liked that bed when I was little. When I was a teenager, I wished for the kind of bed where side curtains could drop down as well. That would have cocooned me from the rest of the family."

Patrick leaned against the doorjamb, watching. Folding his arms across his chest, he studied the room. "I believe this room is larger than the first floor of my house."

Shelby looked over at him in surprise. Then she frowned. "Don't get any ideas, Patrick. This is all show. And the price for it was steep. My grandmother was obsessed with the Beaufort family and Beaufort Hall. She mortgaged it to the hilt. If we ever get it sold, we'll be lucky to get enough to pay all the debts. And you already know what she did to my parents—all in the name of family prestige.''

"Still must be a come-down to be living in my place now.''

"Not a bit. At least there's warmth and a feeling of love in your home. You're giving Mollie something money can't buy, a feeling of being wanted and cherished. I would have given anything to have had that as a child.''

Flushing with the intensity of her words, Shelby turned and wandered to the windows. She had been lucky in her sisters. They had forged a bond that enabled them to endure the loss of their parents and the lack of warmth and love in the huge old family home. At least she'd had that.

"Where's Auntie Georgia's room?'' Mollie asked, sliding down from the bed.

"This way.'' Shelby started from the room, stopping when she reached the door. Patrick was blocking the way. And from the look on his face, he wasn't planning to move any time soon.

"Want to see Georgia's room, too?'' she asked.

"I think I'd like to hear a bit more about Shelby's childhood,'' he said slowly.

"That was a long time ago.''

"Was it so bad?''

"No, not so bad. Especially when we were little like Mollie. I don't think Grandmother wanted to be bothered by little kids, so we had a series of nannies who watched us. We had a lot more freedom then than when we reached our teens. It was then that we started eating meals with Grandmother, and learning proper behavior.

With the intent of attracting the right man and making an advantageous alliance.''

''Advantageous alliance?''

She smiled wryly. ''Her term for marriage.''

''I want to see Auntie Georgia's room, Daddy,'' Mollie said, squeezing between him and the door frame.

''Let it go, Patrick. It was a long time ago. I left as soon as I graduated from high school and only came back once in a while.''

Patrick moved out into the hall. ''We can discuss this further at another time.''

Leading the way across the hall to Georgia's older room, Shelby wondered why he pursued the subject so adamantly.

''Of course, your investigative instincts.''

''What investigative instincts?''

''That's why you want to know more, it's part of some ingrained work ethic because of your job.''

Patrick didn't respond as he watched Shelby show off Georgia's room to his daughter. Wanting to know more about her childhood had nothing to do with being an investigator, he realized. He just plain wanted to know more about Shelby. What made her laugh, or cry. What she'd loved as a child. How she had coped without a mother and father all the times when parents are so important.

He looked around the lavish old home. She'd grown up in luxury. It didn't matter that her grandmother had gone into debt toward the end, Shelby had still been raised with extravagances he could only imagine. And would never have.

It was a good thing their alliance was temporary. He

could never offer to give her a home like this. And sooner or later, she'd want more than he could afford. Hadn't that been one of Sylvia's complaints? She'd wanted him to kill himself slaving away at some high powered law firm, racking up billable hours so money would pour in.

Yet being an investigator was something he loved. He couldn't imagine making a living doing anything else. And, of course, his job was the sole reason Shelby had come into his life—even for a short time.

They explored the second floor until they'd seen into every room. Shelby even led them briefly to the attic to show Patrick where Margot and Rand had found the boxes that also led to their discovery about her father. He listened to all she had to say, trying to read between the words and get a feeling for things unsaid.

As they headed back downstairs, Patrick scooped Mollie up and paused at the head of the stairs.

"This is your chance, Shelby. Go for it."

"What are you talking about?"

"Sliding down the bannister." He found life more fun when trying new things and daring to take chances. Would Shelby feel the same?

She looked at the long expanse of highly polished mahogany, at the steep drop to the side and shook her head.

"Of course if you are some sissy, chicken girl, I guess you can't do it," he teased.

"I'm likely to fall off and break my neck! There was a good reason Grandmother forbid us to even try."

He grinned, and started down the stairs. He'd give her three minutes. He could recognize indecision mixed with desire when he saw it.

"I'll stand beneath the railing and catch you if you fall. You'll probably never have another chance," he called over his shoulder.

Shelby watched as he went down the stairs, but she made no move to take the stairs.

Patrick set Mollie on the marble floor and pointed to the doorway into the living room. "Wait there," he said in a stage whisper, "and watch Shelby."

Walking to stand beneath the highest part of the stairs, he looked up.

He could see her take a breath, and the smile of pure delight that spread.

"Catch me at the bottom," she instructed, as she sat sideways on the wood.

Patrick had no sooner moved to the base of the stairs than she let go a shriek and came sailing down the railing, plunging right into him. She was laughing as they tangled and fell back to the floor. He was glad he'd been there. She'd had no control and could have hurt herself.

Mollie laughed and ran across to kneel beside them. "I want to do that, Daddy. That's fun!"

Patrick slowly sat up, Shelby still in his arms. Her laughter was infectious and he began to chuckle. "Not this time, Mollie. You can't reach the bannister like Shelby can. Maybe when you're older."

"That was wonderful, Patrick. I felt like I was flying."

"I want to fly, Daddy!" Mollie insisted.

Shelby jumped up and reached down a hand for Patrick. "Okay, punkin, we'll see what we can do, right Daddy?"

Patrick didn't release her hand when he rose, but

pulled her closer. "Just how do you propose to do that?"

"She could do it for just a few feet. I'll put her on it and hold her, you catch her at the bottom. It was so much fun I wished I had been able to do it when I was younger. Let's indulge her."

As you were not indulged, Patrick thought, nodding in agreement. "Okay, but only for a few feet."

Mollie loved the sliding and insisted on playing that new game a dozen times more. Patrick finally put his foot down, asking Shelby if she wanted another try.

She shook her head.

"No. That was great. But once was special. To do it again might not be as special. I want to always remember it as it was." She sat on the top step and began to take off her shoes. "But I'll take you up on your other offer."

He nodded and toed off his shoes. But there was another way he wished they could shock her grandmother's ghost, and it had nothing to do with dancing or playing tag.

She rose and shyly looked at him.

He was beginning to understand this complex woman who was his wife. His temporary wife. And that worried him.

"May I have this dance?" he asked with a mock bow.

Mollie stood on the bottom step and clapped her hands. "Dance!"

"With Shelby the first time, okay?"

"Then me."

"Then you."

Patrick swept Shelby into his arms and swooped and

turned and carried them all around the wide foyer. The marble was cool beneath their feet, the humid Mississippi air wafted in from the opened front door. Before long they were both hot and breathless.

Patrick stopped and kissed her. She was warm and smelled heavenly. The taste of her lips was sweet as honey and he wanted her as he hadn't wanted a woman in years. Maybe never.

"My turn," Mollie said, racing across the foyer.

Patrick pulled back, his eyes finding Shelby's. The heat in her cheeks was not all due to their exertion. He recognized the dazed look in her eyes, and something grew inside. He didn't need Shelby's comment on their wedding day to know that she wasn't very experienced. He had only to look into her eyes to see the signs.

"Okay." Patrick reached down to pick up Mollie. He didn't relinquish Shelby's hand even when she tugged.

"We can dance all three," he said.

When he saw the delight in her eyes, he was glad he'd suggested it.

They danced around and around, Mollie shrieking with laughter. Finally, Patrick stopped.

"Enough! It's hot as blazes in here." He put Mollie down and straightened, arching his back and raising his arms over his head to ease some of his muscles. Mollie wasn't growing any lighter as she grew up.

Shelby laughed, and reached out to touch his shoulder. "You're it! Run, Mollie, don't let Daddy get you." With that, Shelby took off toward the dining room, her bare feet slapping against the floor. Mollie was only a step or two behind her.

Patrick hesitated a moment before taking off after

them. He glanced around. "Hope you can see this, Harriet Beaufort. This is what a home is supposed to be like, full of laughter and fun and children running. The things that make happy memories."

Mollie rode in the backseat when they at last headed back for New Orleans. Tired, she soon fell asleep. Shelby was feeling a bit tired herself, but didn't want to miss a single moment of the day. Never imaging the fun that awaited when they left home that morning, she wondered if she'd ever spend such a marvelous day again.

And it was all because of Patrick.

"Did you get enough information from Edith Strong?" she asked, remembering the real reason for the trip.

"I got enough to open a couple of other avenues of inquiry, at least. We'll see where it leads. This takes time."

"I know. And it's not like there's any rush. Margot found out months ago. After more than twenty years, I can't expect him to be easy to find. Especially if he thought the law was after him. He could have changed his name, couldn't he?"

"Yes, and that would make it more difficult. But it's still early, give me some time." Patrick glanced at her. "You're not regretting your bargain, are you? Is Mollie proving a problem?"

"What? Oh, you mean our marriage? No, I'm not sorry we did that. I'm glad I can provide the day care for her. And she's getting better around me. Look at today. In another few weeks, we'll be best friends."

"Just don't get so close you break her heart when you leave."

Shelby nodded. For a while today she'd forgotten she was only a temporary part of their family. Laughing and playing with Mollie and Patrick had been so much fun it was hard to imagine she might not have too many days like this. Once Patrick discovered where her father was, his side of the agreement would be fulfilled. And once Margot had her baby and Mollie was eligible for after-school care, Shelby would no longer be needed. She would be on her own again.

Patrick was right to warn her not to get too involved. Mollie wasn't the only one who could have her heart broken.

Keeping the business nature of their relationship in the forefront of her mind, Shelby tried to build some reserve into her dealings with Patrick and Mollie. Sunday she declined their offer to join them at the park, pleading the need to do laundry, grocery shopping and maybe even get to some of the work Patrick had brought home on Friday night.

But she couldn't help feeling left out when they departed.

Knowing she could have gone didn't ease the sensation, but working around the small house helped. She took pride in caring for Patrick's things, and her own. When the house was spotless, the laundry put away and the grocery list made, she sat down for a few moments' rest before heading out to the store.

Impulsively, she dialed Georgia's number. Her sister answered on the second ring.

"What's up?" she asked when she heard it was Shelby.

"Not much. Patrick took Mollie to the park and I'm going shopping soon. I wanted to thank you and your friends for moving my things. Everything looked perfect when we got here."

"So you said on the message you left last Monday. Sorry I missed your call. Work is frantic. But in a few weeks, I'm due for some vacation. Can I use it!"

"Your training program will be over by then?"

"Yes. So the timing is perfect. I'll take my vacation and then ask for a permanent assignment to the emergency room when I return. If St. Joe can't do it, I might put out feelers to some of the other hospitals. I really want to do this type of nursing. How's my favorite niece?"

Shelby smiled. "She's your only one so far and only by marriage."

"If Margot has a boy, she'll still be my only one—and favorite."

"Don't get too attached," Shelby said.

"Why not?"

Oops. "Well, if Margot has a girl, you might want to make her your favorite."

"If that happens, I won't have favorites. I wish she and Rand would agree to find out ahead of time."

"I like it that we won't know until the baby is born."

They chatted for a few minutes. When she hung up, Shelby felt better. She would always have her sisters, even when her marriage to Patrick ended. And there was nothing saying she and Georgia and Margot couldn't continue to see Mollie from time to time.

Of course that would mean seeing Patrick, too. Which wouldn't be all bad, she thought as she headed out to shop.

Since the Fourth of July holiday had the garages closed Monday, Shelby's car was still not fixed when she went to work on Tuesday, so Patrick drove her, stopping in to see the child care facilities which Mollie proudly showed off.

Shelby almost asked him to stop by her office so she could show *him* off.

She caught herself before she could ask. Where was the distance she was trying to put between them?

Her car was repaired by the end of the day and Patrick arranged to have it delivered to the office. She was touched by his thoughtful gesture, but she secretly wished he had picked them up.

Wednesday he didn't call her at the office as had been his habit the previous week. Shelby missed the calls, but had only herself to blame. She had wanted the distance between them, so she shouldn't complain that it was working.

Thursday afternoon Patrick called Shelby at work.

"Is something wrong?" she asked. Last week he'd called before lunch each day. This week, he'd been too busy. Or at least that's what he'd told her last night when she mentioned it at dinner.

"One of my operatives is sick. We've been working on a suspected insurance fraud for your firm. Which includes someone watching him around the clock. Since Mel is sick, I'll need to take the night shift. Can you manage all right at home alone?"

"Sure. This is one of the reasons you married me,

remember, so I can be there for Mollie when something like this happens. No problem. We get along fine these days. Will you be home at all tonight?''

''Probably not. I'll swing by the house in a few minutes and pick up a few things—something to read and some soft drinks to keep me going. Tomorrow I'll be able to pull rank and assign someone else, but this caught me by surprise.''

''No problem. This isn't dangerous, is it?''

''No. The man swears he injured his back and can hardly walk. The doctors can find no evidence of trauma, but there is the possibility he's telling the truth. That's what we're hoping to find out. No danger.''

''Okay, then I'll see you tomorrow after work, I guess.''

Shelby treated Mollie to dinner at one of her favorite fast food places—the one where there was play equipment. Mollie entertained herself for an hour on all the climbing gear and bouncing balls.

The house was silent when Shelby let them in. She quickly got Mollie ready for bed, read her a long story, and tucked her in for the night. Then she wandered into the living room. There were no new folders or stacks of papers. Patrick had obviously not brought any work home to leave for her.

His new temporary help was proving adaptable and able to keep up with the day-to-day routine. And the backlog was almost caught up, he'd told her Tuesday.

She switched on the television, aware of how much she missed Patrick.

''This will never do, what happens when the marriage ends?'' Shelby asked herself as she flipped through the different channels. Nothing appealed. She switched it off.

The phone rang.

Margot was on the other end.

"Hi, how's married life?"

"Great," Shelby forced enthusiasm into her tone.

"Rand and I want to watch Mollie this weekend. Give you and Patrick another night alone."

She and Patrick alone in the house? Shelby's imagination kicked in and she smiled at the thought. Maybe they could dance barefoot like they had in Natchez. The memory of his kiss at Beaufort Hall surfaced. That she'd like even better. Frowning when she realized where her thoughts were leading, she shook her head. That would never do!

"I don't know. She can be fairly rambunctious."

"We loved having her before. She's a delight. Besides, Rand will be here and it will be good practice for us. We'll have one of our own in a few months, remember?"

"And you need to rest!"

"Phooey, I'm feeling great. I had a checkup earlier this week and everything looks perfect. Come on, let Mollie come visit. You and Patrick deserve some time alone. You are still newlyweds."

"I'll check with him and let you know."

"I'll hold. Ask him now so we'll know for sure."

"Actually, he's out on a stakeout tonight," Shelby said slowly. "He won't be home until tomorrow." And, she just realized, she had no way to reach him.

"Ask first thing and let us know. You two could go out to dinner and dancing and then return home and be alone all weekend."

"I'll check and let you know. Thanks, Margot, this is really great."

Shelby continued to feel like a fraud, and wondered if Margot could detect it in her tone. The last thing she wanted was to be alone with Patrick. Wasn't she trying to build a reserve between them to guard her heart?

Guard her heart?

Was she growing fond of Patrick?

Falling in love with the man?

No! He was searching for her father and she was just a temporary mother for Mollie. There was nothing more involved.

"Tell me what the doctor said," Shelby said in an effort to escape her tumultuous thoughts.

She envied Margot's happiness and assurance of her husband's love. Would Shelby ever find a strong love to bind her through eternity?

After talking with Margot, Shelby felt restless. She decided to take a long soak in the tub to settle down for bed. She had the house to herself and nothing pressing to do.

Checking on Mollie before running the water, she felt her heart melt a bit more at the sight of the enchanting little girl. Kissing her softly on her cheek, Shelby felt a wealth of love well up.

She wished she could be around to see Mollie grow. When would she give up her teddy bear? Would she ever give up her baseball cap, or stop saying gots? How would she like school in the fall? She played well with the other children in day care, and already had made friends. Shelby envied her that. Shyness was such an awkward trait.

Feeling indulgent, Shelby dumped in fragrant bath

salts when she ran the water for her bath. She found a
bunch of candles and lit a dozen, enjoying the soft glow
of candlelight as she slipped into the silken hot water.
Leaning back, she closed her eyes, letting her thoughts
drift as she relaxed.

She'd enjoy the hot bath until the water grew cold,
then go to bed and start that new book she'd bought.
She'd left the door open, though Mollie usually slept
through the night. But she was in charge with Patrick
gone and didn't want to take any chances the little girl
would wake up and be scared if Shelby didn't hear her
call immediately.

The water soothed, its warmth seeping into her, re-
laxing her. If she began to feel sleepy, she'd have to
get out, but until then, it was nice to just drift.

"I wondered what was causing the flickering light,"
Patrick said from the doorway.

Shelby sat straight up in startled shock.

"What are you doing here?" she cried. Snatching
the washrag, she held it in front of her. It wasn't big
enough. Heat seeped through her that had nothing to
do with the water.

"I live here," he said with amusement.

"I thought you were going to be gone all night."
She was conscious of his gaze moving across her.
Shifting the washcloth, she tried to vainly to cover
more of her bare skin.

"And this is how you indulge yourself when I'm
gone?" he said, a slow smile lighting his face as he let
his gaze trail over her.

"Get out, Patrick."

"I'm not really in, just standing here in the doorway."

"Close the door—with you on the outside," she snapped, feeling twice as hot under his eyes. Why hadn't she used bubble bath so she could sink beneath the bubbles and at least maintain a modicum of modesty? Or closed the door and taken the chance Mollie wouldn't wake?

Or just take a quick shower for all that?

Instead of doing as she ordered, Patrick pushed away and stepped into the dimly lit room. Squatting beside the tub, he leaned over and kissed her soft lips.

"You are so beautiful," he said softly, kissing her again.

Despite common sense arguing against it, Shelby reached up one hand to his neck and held on while Patrick deepened the kiss.

"You shouldn't be here," she whispered a minute later when he pulled back and gazed into her eyes. Her heart raced. She could scarcely breathe.

"I told you, I live here."

"What happened to the stakeout?"

He laughed and stood up. "The guy blew it. Some friend drove up in this fancy car and the man just about did a jig looking it over. I have almost an entire roll of film showing him with no apparent impediment to normal living. More than enough for the insurance company. So I came home. I didn't notice that you left the door open when you bathed before."

"I did it to hear Mollie if she woke. Would you please let me have a bit of privacy so I can get out and dressed?"

He shrugged. "If you insist."

"I do!"

He sauntered to the door, and glanced over his shoulder. "I could help," he said audaciously.

"Get out!"

Laughing, Patrick complied, pulling the door shut behind him.

"Come and sit with me while I eat," he called.

Shelby wanted to sink beneath the water and hide, but knew that was a vain thought. She couldn't stay in the bathroom forever.

But all relaxation fled. She felt tight as a drawn bowstring. Rising quickly, she dried off and donned her light gown and robe. Blowing out the candles, she brushed her hair and debated what to do. She had to face the man sometime. Might as well get it over with. Taking a deep breath, she headed reluctantly for the kitchen.

She refused to be embarrassed. They were married. He'd been married before, and had seen it all, she was sure. Yet she couldn't help feel flustered when she stepped inside and Patrick turned and smiled wickedly at her.

"Next time, maybe I'll join you."

CHAPTER EIGHT

SHELBY ignored the suggestive comment and crossed to the refrigerator. If she could bluff away her embarrassment, maybe he wouldn't tease her.

"Shall I make you something hot to eat, or would a sandwich and salad do?"

"Anything. I got a burger late this afternoon, but I'm hungry now. How did it go with Mollie?"

"Fine." She quickly prepared him a roast beef sandwich, and tossed a small green salad. Setting both before him at the small breakfast table, she returned to the counter to put away the food, avoiding his eyes.

"Stop fussing and come sit with me," Patrick said around a mouthful of sandwich.

Shelby looked at him, drawn like a moth to the flame. She loved being with him, enjoyed hearing him talk. Found his way of thinking fascinating, and different. She'd never spent so much time with a man before. She liked it.

Afraid of the trend of her thoughts, she pulled out a chair and sat. Not too close, but near enough she could reach out and touch him—if she dared.

"Tell me about the case. Did the man know you saw him? Did you get enough proof?"

"He never knew I was there. I need to make sure the film is developed properly before confronting him. But I'm sure the scam will end tomorrow. Saves the insurance company a ton of money."

"Which means a healthy fee for you, right?"

"Healthy enough. This is good, but you look good enough to eat," he said, sampling the salad.

Flustered, Shelby sought another topic of conversation. "Margot called tonight. She and Rand offered to watch Mollie this weekend."

"Why?"

Shelby winced. Maybe the reasons weren't so good. This topic could lead back to the one she'd been trying to avoid.

"Actually, she said it was to get some practice. For when her baby comes."

Patrick bit into the sandwich again and studied her. "There's more."

She wrinkled her nose. "No wonder you're so good at your job. You never take anything at face value. Actually," Shelby hesitated, then rushed into speech, "she thought it would give us a weekend alone. To go to dinner or something."

Slowly his eyes lit up. Then he smiled.

Shelby didn't trust that smile.

"What?"

"I think Margot's offer is brilliant. I'm sure Mollie will love visiting them. Tell them I appreciate the offer."

"We don't have to go out to dinner, that was just her idea."

"And a good one. Dinner and dancing. Though not with bare feet like at Beaufort Hall, maybe." Patrick finished his sandwich. "And with Mollie gone, we don't have to worry about making noise in the night, or getting up early. We could sleep in as long as we wanted."

"Making noise in the night?"

Patrick leaned over and drew Shelby from her chair, into his lap. His hands held her loosely, but Shelby knew if she made a move to leave, he'd clamp down.

His gaze caught hers and he leaned closer. "Sometimes when people make love they make noise. Have you thought about what I asked on our wedding day?"

Shelby blinked and tried to look away, but she was mesmerized by the hot longing clearly evident in Patrick's gaze. The wash of desire that swept through surprised her. She wanted to say yes, but her innate caution held her back.

"I still don't think it's a good idea to get involved that way."

"Aren't you tempted the least little bit?"

She sighed and leaned against him. "I never stop thinking about it," she confessed.

With an exclamation of triumph, he kissed her, his mouth capturing hers in a manner designed to drive her out of her mind. He moved his hand over her back, around to cup one breast through her robe and gown. Her heart kicked in double time and the world seemed to spin out of control.

"Patrick, stop!" She pushed back and stood up, breathing hard. Staring at him Shelby knew she'd like nothing more than to fling herself into his arms and never have him stop kissing her.

But she wanted more than just physical pleasure. She wanted caring and affection. Love.

"Now what?" he asked, leaning back in his chair and tucking his fingers in the pockets of his trousers. His expression was impassive, giving nothing away.

"Nothing has changed. We agreed to marry so you'd

look for my father. Now you want to change the rules. That's not fair."

"It is if both of us agree. You've just said you never stop thinking about it."

"But that doesn't mean I want to…to give into…"

Patrick came to his feet. "Say what you mean, Shelby."

She shook her head. She wasn't sure what she meant, but maybe it would be better if he thought she was just rejecting him. She only had so much willpower and he tested it every time he came near her.

"I get the picture," he said coolly. "I won't trouble you again." With that he strode from the room.

Shelby watched him leave, heard his step on the stairs.

"Great job, Shelby. Now you've really done it." Slowly she took his plates to the sink and rinsed them. How could she tell him the truth? He'd suspect she was angling for just what she was trying to avoid. Yet she hated him thinking she didn't want him.

But they had no future together. Hadn't he made it clear he was not interested in a permanent relationship again? She wasn't sure what had happened in his first marriage, but whatever it had been sure made him wary around women. It had taken him two days after she made her outlandish offer before he could bring himself to accept—and she knew he had only done so in order to keep Mollie.

Nothing had changed. Sighing softly, she turned off the light and went up to bed. But sleep was a long time coming.

Margot called Shelby at work the Friday morning.

"Hi, I won't talk long, just wondered if you've spoken with Patrick yet?''

"Yes. He said he appreciated the invitation," Shelby said slowly.

"Great. We thought we'd stop by today and get her. That would give you an extra night. And you could sleep in late two mornings in a row. I bet that sounds like heaven, right?''

Shelby gripped the receiver. Great, she'd have two nights with Patrick's cool manner and distant attitude instead of one and with no Mollie there to act as a buffer. Yet she couldn't say anything to Margot without worrying her.

"Are you sure this won't be too much for you? I thought you were supposed to take things easy?''

"Don't be a worrywart. I'm fine. And Mollie is a doll. We plan to go to the park, and then maybe rent some Disney videos and pop corn. She'll have a ball."

"Ummm."

"Something wrong?''

"Nothing!" Shelby answered immediately. "When did you want her to be ready?'' She saw no way to avoid the visit. No way to avoid being with Patrick for two whole days.

"We'll stop by at six. That'll give you time to get home and pack a few things for her, won't it?''

"Yes. See you then.''

As she hung up the phone, Shelby wondered if she could insist Mollie return early Sunday morning. No, that would defeat Margot's gesture. Sighing, she wished she had never gotten into such a tangle. She still wanted to know about her father, but wondered if the price would prove too high.

That evening after Mollie left with Margot and Rand, Shelby busied herself preparing the grill she'd found in Patrick's garage. She'd much rather barbeque outside than be confined in the small kitchen alone with Patrick. Especially after last night.

She had the coals glowing and a fruit salad prepared when he came home. He had a stack of folders in a large case. Obviously he, too, planned to keep things businesslike.

Shelby explained that Mollie had already left for the Marstalls' and would be home sometime Sunday afternoon. Patrick nodded and headed for the living room, telling her to call him when dinner was ready.

She missed the companionship they had shared during the past two weeks while she prepared dinner. She missed Mollie's chatter as well. It was lonely and quiet.

"Better get used to it, girl," she muttered as she rotated the chicken on the grill. As soon as their mock marriage ended, she'd be alone again. Again Shelby wondered if she would ever find anyone to love, to build a life with.

Someone with a quick mind, a bit unconventional, who could kiss like every fantasy ever invented.

Someone like Patrick.

Ruthlessly squelching her thoughts, she speared a drumstick, and lifted it to the platter. Time to eat and stop thinking!

No thinking was easier said than done, Shelby admitted later that evening.

Dinner had been quick and impersonal. Patrick ate, left the table and resumed the work he'd brought home. It didn't take long to clean the plates. Then Shelby was at a loose end.

In the past she might have called a friend or one of her sisters, but anyone she called tonight would find it extremely odd that a newly wed woman didn't want to spend time with her husband.

Maybe she shouldn't have conspired to keep the truth of the situation quiet from her sister. Or enlisted others in the deception. It was hard to carry the burden alone.

Not quite alone. Patrick shared it with her.

Drying her hands, Shelby headed for the living room. She could help him with the office work. She'd done quite a bit over the last couple of weeks, and knew exactly what he expected in that area. It was in the personal arena she wasn't so certain.

He looked up when she stepped into the room, a look of inquiry on his face.

"I thought I could help," she said, feeling flustered again. Darn, she thought she was beyond that. After all, she'd done nothing wrong. She wasn't the one trying to change the rules in midstream.

"This is the last of the backlog. If I can get it all caught up by the end of the weekend, then things will be back to normal at the office. I offered the temp a permanent job today. She's going to let me know on Monday. If she stays, she can learn the rest of the procedures. So far she's a hard worker and keeps up with the day-to-day load."

"Good." Shelby took a folder and began to read.

Except for the odd tension that seemed to hum between them, the evening was not very different from others they'd shared. Patrick worked diligently through the files, scanning reports, checking the billing records, and jotting notes on a sheet of paper where he wanted to do further follow-up.

Shelby looked up to watch him every time she finished with a folder. He looked tired. Her heart lurched. Was he working too hard? She knew that, despite the work of his two operatives, things had fallen behind when he'd had the difficulty with Mollie's day care, but surely things were getting better there now. That was her contribution.

"Why don't you go up to bed, Patrick," she said when the clock chimed ten. "You look tired."

He shrugged, but didn't raise his gaze from the folder on his lap.

"You have all day tomorrow to work on these folders."

"No, I have an assignment tomorrow."

"Oh." So much for Margot's brilliant idea of giving them time together.

He looked up. After a minute, he said, "Want to go with me?"

Shelby didn't hesitate. "I'd love to. Are you going undercover?"

"You've been watching too many TV private eye shows. There is rarely a need to go undercover in my line of work."

"Okay, so what are you doing tomorrow?"

"Watching a place in the Quarter to see if we can spot who's been passing counterfeit bills."

"Isn't that something the cops would do?"

"They have a stakeout, but the owner suspects a member of his extended family and if he can discover who's doing it before the cops, he might be able to minimize the fallout."

Shelby gazed off into space, envisioning her and Patrick on a case together. Smiling, she realized once again he'd thrown her off balance. And offered her a chance at something extraordinary.

"Thanks, Patrick. This will be fun."

"It'll probably be tedious, boring and get old real fast. But if you're game, we leave at nine."

Shelby jumped up. "I better get to bed, then, so I can get up early and be ready to go. What should I wear?"

"Whatever you usually do if you're browsing around the Quarter. The key here is to make sure you don't look obvious." He stacked the folders and held his hand for the one she'd been working on. She brought it over almost dancing with excitement. This would be fun! And give her time with Patrick.

He rose and switched off the lamp. When he turned, he almost bumped into Shelby.

She flung her arms around him and hugged him tightly. "Thanks. This will be so different, but exciting, don't you think?"

He resisted with every ounce of willpower he possessed. She hadn't a clue how difficult she made it for him to keep the distance he'd vowed to keep after last night. She wasn't interested, end of subject. Once he found her father, she'd be gone and wanted no complications to confuse the issue.

But it didn't feel like the end of the subject with her soft body pressed against his, with her arms holding him tightly. And her smile was enough to melt icebergs. How was one man to resist?

She almost had him considering extending the end of the relationship beyond what they'd agreed to, but he knew how that went. Hadn't he learned from Sylvia that he wasn't cut out for marriage? He had his daughter and once she was in school, they could establish a routine that would see them through the years until she was grown and on her own.

Shelby stepped back, dropping her arms. "Good night," she said and turned to hurry to the stairs.

Patrick watched her go, feeling old and tired and lonely.

By five o'clock the next afternoon, Shelby was ready to throw in the towel. She had been pretending to be shopping at one store in the French Quarter all day! Fortunately it was large and had an extensive inventory. Nevertheless she felt she could itemize everything in the place from the lovely ceramic masks, to the elaborate be-feathered Mardi Gras masks to the tacky souvenirs lining the shelves right inside the door. Somehow the work of a private investigator seemed more glamorous on television.

Patrick showed none of the boredom he must be feeling. He looked as fresh and alert as he had when he first introduced her to the store owner that morning, explaining she was a new trainee.

"Ready to leave?"

She jumped. She hadn't seen him walk over to her. Some private investigator she'd make.

"Yes." She hoped her enthusiasm wasn't too obvious.

Patrick called a good night to the owner and took Shelby's arm, leading her to the street. "Want to get a bite to eat before we head for home?"

"Sure. Do you do this kind of thing a lot? It was a

very long day." She rotated one foot then the other to ease the ache.

"I used to when I was starting out. Now I have others who have less experience and can use the training. But every once in a while I like to do some field work myself. Keeps the edge, you know."

"Ummm. I wonder if the owner will ever find out who is passing the phoney money," she said as they walked along Royal Street, heading toward Canal Street.

"Just a matter of time. And careful surveillance."

As they reached busy Canal Street, one of the riverboats' whistles blew.

"Let's go see," she said impulsively. She loved watching the old stern wheelers move with stately grace up and down the river. She remembered watching them as a child in Natchez.

"We could see if there's room on the dinner cruise, have dinner aboard, if you like," Patrick said as they sauntered in the late afternoon heat. "It'd be cooler on the river."

Shelby hesitated. It seemed too much like what Margot had suggested, dinner and dancing at some romantic restaurant. What could be more romantic than a riverboat dinner cruise? Still, if Patrick hadn't wanted to do it, he wouldn't have suggested it.

"I'd like that."

The stern wheeler was crowded when they stepped aboard. Saturday nights combined locals with tourists. But the festive feeling was infectious. In no time, Shelby regained energy and her enthusiasm. Forgotten was the long day on her feet. When the Dixieland music started, she tapped out the rhythm with her toe.

"You like Dixieland?" Patrick leaned closer to ask.

She nodded, smiling brightly. "When I was a little girl, we'd hear the music from some of the boats as they moved up river. It sounded so bright and exciting. Grandmother never let it in her home. She preferred the classics."

"Then, I'm glad we came." He enjoyed the look of pure bliss on her face. And it made it a lot easier to resist Shelby's allure with a couple of hundred other passengers around. He glanced at his watch. Another eighteen hours and Mollie would be home.

He could last until then. When she was home, she made the perfect shield against anything personal developing between him and Shelby.

Dinner proved to be enjoyable. They shared a table with a couple from Texas and spent the meal exchanging stories about New Orleans and Dallas. When the last of the dessert had been consumed, Patrick took Shelby to the aft lounge to listen to the soft jazz that was playing. Finding a couple of chairs near a dark corner, he put them together and sat beside her.

By the time the riverboat returned to the dock, Patrick was ready to swim ashore. The cold river water would be perfect to quench the fire ignited by Shelby's presence. She did nothing that could be construed as provocative, unless he counted her breathing. But it didn't take much, he was coming to realize. He enjoyed her company, liked to find what made her laugh, and dare her to try different things. She always seemed so naively startled to find she could do something she had not tried before. He was growing cynical and it was refreshing to be with someone who was still wide-eyed and fascinated about the world.

It was late by the time they reached home. But Patrick was too keyed up to sleep. He bid Shelby good-night once they were inside and headed for the living room. There were still a few more records to get straight.

"Aren't you going to bed now?" she asked, pausing by the bottom step.

"I'll be up later."

"Thanks, Patrick. This was a most interesting day."

He looked at her, struck by her tone. "But not one you want to repeat too often."

Hesitating a moment, she remembered the excitement that he was sharing a part of himself with her. That she'd liked. But she wrinkled her nose and slowly shook her head. "I don't think so. My feet still ache and if I never see a souvenir of New Orleans again, it'll be too soon. I wish we could have caught the bad guy, though."

"We'll get him. Or the cops will. But it was a perfect day for showing you what a lot of my business is like. Next time, I'll wait until I have some surveillance going where we sit in the car all night."

"Please do. Thanks for taking me today. I liked the ending," she said as she turned to run lightly up the stairs.

He would have liked the ending more if he were going up with her, he thought wryly. He leaned against the archway into the living room and just listened. He heard Shelby enter the bathroom—and firmly close the door behind her. For a moment the memory of her in the bath flashed into mind. Guess there wouldn't be any more nights where she bathed by candlelight. At least not while he was home.

A few minutes later he heard her cross the hall to her room, and again close the door. Shaking his head, he pushed off from the wall and headed for the small stack of folders that waited. If he couldn't sleep, he might as well be productive!

Shelby knew she'd blown it. Sunday morning and here she sat sipping coffee alone. Idly she twisted around the muffin she nibbled on. She wasn't hungry. Sipping the coffee was about the limit of her interest in sustenance.

Patrick walked in and when she looked up, she caught her breath. He'd obviously just finished his shower. His hair was still damp, and his face freshly shaved. The echo of the words he'd once said to her applied here. *He looked good enough to eat!*

He pulled out a chair, turned it around and straddled it, resting his arms on the high back.

"Mollie will be home soon," he said.

She nodded.

"I expect Margot and Rand will bring her in."

"I guess so."

"Which means we'll have to play our charade again. Just wanted to make sure that's what you wanted."

Licking her lip, Shelby nodded. "If you don't mind."

Patrick shook his head, his eyes boring into hers. "Once your sister's gone, I thought I'd take Mollie swimming. We'll be out of your hair this afternoon."

Shelby's heart sank. He didn't even want to be around her. Maybe she should throw caution to the wind and agree to his suggestion. It couldn't hurt any more than if she didn't. She was fast falling in love with the man. Maybe she should grab for whatever happiness she could find and let the future take care of itself.

Only, now, she didn't have a clue how to bring it up. He hadn't mentioned it again. Had he changed his mind?

"You two don't have to leave on my account."

He shrugged. "It's no hardship. Mollie likes to swim. Want us to get dinner out?"

"No! I've already planned dinner."

She wished he'd invite her to go swimming with them. But apparently the conversation was over. He rose, replaced the chair and left.

Feeling inadequate and dejected, Shelby rose and went to dress for the day. Maybe between now and the time they left, Patrick would invite her to join them.

He didn't.

Rand brought Mollie home, explaining that Margot was feeling tired and he'd insisted she stay in bed.

"I thought watching Mollie would be too much," Shelby said, worried for her sister.

"No, it wasn't. We had a great time. But Margot and I were up late last night and I just thought she should rest today. We'd like to have Mollie come stay with us again sometime soon."

"Maybe after your own baby is born," Patrick said. They all were at the front door, Rand having declined to enter.

"We'll want to have her visit again long before that," Rand said, before turning to head for his car.

"Have fun, kid?" Patrick asked.

Mollie exuberantly explained her visit. Before Shelby could hear all she had to say, Patrick suggested swimming, which immediately changed the direction of Mollie's thoughts. She ran upstairs to find her bathing suit and in only moments, she and her father had left.

Shelby watched them drive away. He hadn't asked her. And she hadn't invited herself along. Now what was she going to do for the rest of the day? Dinner wouldn't take long to prepare. She could do laundry and vacuum the house, but the feeling of belonging she'd experienced last week was missing.

She wanted to be with Patrick, pure and simple.

The following Wednesday Shelby was about at the end of her rope. Any thought of keeping her distance from Patrick had long since faded. And yet she was unable to draw closer. It was as if he'd erected an invisible wall between them. Nothing she said seemed to breach it.

Maybe plain speaking was called for. Tonight she'd wait until Mollie was in bed, and then tell Patrick she'd changed her mind. She didn't want to continue as they had over the last two days. If he still wanted her, then—

When the phone rang, Shelby snatched it up. She kept hoping the next call would be Patrick. It wasn't. It was Mrs. Robinson at the day care.

"Mrs. O'Shaunnessy, we need you down here. There's been an accident."

CHAPTER NINE

"AN accident? What happened?" Fear clutched her.

"I'm afraid Mollie fell and cut herself quite badly. We've called for an ambulance but she's asking for her father. Can you notify him and then come down?"

"I'll be there in two minutes."

Quickly Shelby hung up, then picked up the phone and dialed Patrick's work number from memory. The temp answered. What was her name? Shelby couldn't remember.

"I need to speak with Patrick, please. It's an emergency," she said, already rising and walking around her desk. As soon as she told him, she'd be ready to dash for the elevator.

"He's not available right now. What happened? Can I take a message? I'll try to locate him."

"Tell him his wife called. There's been an accident and Mollie's been hurt. I'm going with her to the hospital. I'll call him from there." Shelby slammed down the receiver and ran for the door.

When she entered the day care facility a couple of minutes later she spotted Mollie immediately. One of the teachers held her, pressing a white cloth to her head. The little girl was crying, calling for her daddy. Blood had splattered over her play suit and along the side of her head.

Shelby almost burst into tears at the sight.

"Oh, Mollie, honey, what happened?" She reached for her and Mollie lunged into her arms.

"Shelby, I gots hurt."

"I can see that, honey. What happened?" She raised her gaze to the teacher.

"She was playing on the slide and took a tumble over the side. We found some rocks on the playground, think one of them caused the gash. She'll be fine, but we have called an ambulance. She needs to be checked out by a doctor to make sure."

"Shh, honey, I know it hurts, but you're going to be all right," Shelby crooned as she hugged Mollie tightly and rocked her back and forth. The little girl continued to cry, but she stopped calling for her father and snuggled against Shelby's breasts.

"I'm glad you comed, Shelby. I was a-scared."

"Of course I came, darling. As soon as they called me. I'm so sorry you were hurt. Your daddy will be here as soon as he can."

In a whirlwind of activity they were transported to Liberty Hospital. The young doctor in the emergency room soon had Mollie cleaned up and placed two small stitches in the gash near her hairline.

Giving her a tetanus shot, he pronounced her fit as a fiddle.

"Or she will be in a couple of days. I expect she'll be achy and show some bruises. But this kind of thing happens all the time with kids. Don't worry, Mrs. O'Shaunnessy, she'll be fine. How are you doing?"

Shelby nodded and tried to respond intelligently, but she felt shaky.

"Shelby?" a familiar voice roared.

"In here, Patrick," she called, moving to peer through the opening in the curtain. "We're in here."

She was so glad to see him when he walked in.

"Daddy!" Mollie called, struggling to sit up on the high examination table.

"Easy, kiddo." The doctor assisted her to sit and Patrick swept her into his arms.

"Is she okay?" he asked the doctor.

"She'll be fine. I was telling your wife, she'll be achy for a few days and probably sport some colorful bruises, but there is no concussion, no broken bones."

Patrick turned and saw Shelby. Without a word, he crossed to her and put his free arm around her shoulders, pulling her tightly against him.

She gave way and leaned into his strength. It felt so good!

"I'm sorry, Patrick. She fell on the playground."

"This kind of thing happens with kids, honey. Not your fault. How are you doing? You're as pale as a ghost."

"I'm fine. Do you suppose they weren't watching her closely at the day care?"

"No, what I think is this is just one of a long line of accidents we're likely to face as she grows up. I had my share of visits to the emergency room and doctor's office as a kid, didn't you?"

Shelby shook her head.

Patrick tightened his grip. "Well, if your grandmother hadn't constrained you so much you would have! Are we ready to go?" He looked at the doctor.

The man wrote a prescription, ripped the sheet off the pad and held it out. "Get this filled and give some to Mollie if she complains about headaches. Otherwise, keep her quiet for a day or two. She'll be fine. Have her regular doctor see her in a week. The stitches will be ready to come out by then.''

''Thanks.''

Shelby reluctantly turned from the comfort of Patrick's embrace and tried to smile at the young doctor. But her heart raced as she followed Patrick. Adrenaline let-down, she tried to tell herself as they left the hospital.

They headed for Patrick's car. He spoke softly to Mollie as she rested her head against his shoulder. Shelby felt totally helpless. And guilty. Maybe the child care situation at her work wasn't safe. Had she put Mollie in danger by offering that solution to Patrick?

Once settled in the car, Patrick glanced at her as he started the engine. ''You okay?''

She nodded. ''I was so scared.''

''Yeah, so was I the first couple of times.''

Shelby swung her head around to stare at him in startled surprise. *''The first couple of times?''*

He pulled out of the parking lot and merged with the flow of traffic. ''Adventuresome kids get into trouble. Fact of life. But when she first came to live with me, I didn't know it. She skinned her knees when she was trying to race one of the kids in the neighborhood. I wanted to forbid her to ever set foot out of her room—at least until she was thirty or something. To keep her safe, you know?''

Shelby nodded.

''But that's unrealistic. Joanne at work, who is the mother of three boys, set me straight. When Mollie's finger was smashed by a neighbor's child, I was able to handle it much better. But I have to tell you, you never get completely complacent about it.''

''She's so little. Maybe she shouldn't go on slides yet. Do you think the day care is a mistake? Maybe I should stay home and watch her.''

He flicked her a quick look. ''No, you don't. She's fine at day care. She loves playing with the other children. Think how much she talks about them at dinner every night. She'll be fine, Shelby.''

Checking on Mollie, Shelby blinked away tears. The little girl looked so small in the backseat. The bandage was a stark white on her head. Dirt and blood had stained her clothes. She was fast asleep.

''Hey,'' Patrick reached out to take Shelby's hand. ''She'll be fine. Welcome to the world of parenting.''

''I think you should reconsider your idea of keeping her in her room until she's thirty. Sounds pretty good to me.''

He chuckled and squeezed gently. ''You'll toughen up.''

Shelby doubted it. Even if she had time. But in all likelihood she'd be gone from their lives before the next mishap occurred.

Despite being scared to death when she ran into that day care center this afternoon, Shelby knew she'd miss being a part of Mollie's life—no matter what happened.

The warmth from Patrick's hand began to seep into her. He had the ability to make her forget everything. She wondered how far along he'd gotten in his search for her father. If it took forever, that would probably suit her.

What if he never did?

Instead of the old familiar frustration at not knowing

more about her father, Shelby began to imagine he was lost forever. And she'd stay with Patrick until they were both old and gray. Every few months he'd come home and tell her that he still had no clues. She'd have to pretend to care. But the truth was, the quest had taken a backseat to what was important to her now.

She still felt shaky. Maybe her emotions were too suspect. She couldn't be falling in love with Patrick!

When they reached the house, Patrick scooped Mollie up and carried her up the sidewalk.

"I'll give her a bath and put her down for a nap," he said as Shelby unlocked the front door.

"I can help."

"No need. You'll want to get cleaned up yourself. I can manage." He strode up the stairs, carrying his daughter as if she weighed nothing.

Shelby watched them, once again feeling left out. Was she always going to be on the outside looking in?

Using the downstairs powder room to wash, she then went to her room to don a cool dress and slip into sandals. She felt exhausted. Hearing their laughter reassured her as nothing else had. Mollie *would* be all right.

But would she?

Shelby peeked into the door to Molly's room, watching silently as Patrick rocked Mollie in his arms. He was so big, and the little girl looked particularly small when cradled in her daddy's arms. Love blossomed in Shelby's heart as she studied the two of them. There was something special about a strong man holding a child so tenderly.

"Is she all right?" she asked when Patrick noticed her in the doorway.

"Almost asleep," he said.

Mollie smiled sleepily at Shelby.

It was at that moment Shelby realized she couldn't love Mollie any more if she were her own child. Raising her gaze to Patrick, she knew without a doubt she loved them both.

"I'll start dinner," she said and turned to flee. If only she could outrun her emotions.

"Dumb move, Shelby," she said a few minutes later as she drew the meat from the refrigerator. "Patrick's made it clear more than once that he's not in this for the long haul."

"What are you muttering about?" Patrick asked as he walked into the kitchen.

He hadn't heard, had he? Shelby eyed him warily. "Nothing, just mumbling. She asleep?"

"Yes. And as late as it is, she might sleep through the night."

"She didn't get any dinner."

"She'll ask for something if she gets hungry. I think sleep is better for her right now."

Patrick pulled out a chair and sat down with a tired sigh. Stretching out his long legs, he tilted back on the rear legs of the chair and slipped his hands in his pockets. "Mollie was glad you showed up when I didn't."

"She kept calling for you, they said, but she stopped when I got there. Not quite the same as her daddy, but an adequate substitute, I guess."

"No doubt about it. Thanks. I owe you."

Shelby shook her head. "Just my job, right?"

Patrick was silent for a long time. "Yeah, I guess."

She looked over at his tone, but he appeared lost in thought. Worried about his daughter, she suspected.

* * *

Dinner was quiet without Mollie's chatter. Once finished, Patrick offered to help with the dishes.

"Not necessary. There are only a few, I'll be done in no time," Shelby said, rising to clear the table.

At loose ends, he wandered outside. Turning on the sprinklers, he watched as the water caught the waning light of the setting sun, showering rainbows everywhere. Feeling restless and unsettled, he didn't want to watch television. Might as well watch the water spray.

He had not brought any more work home. They were caught up, thanks to Shelby's assistance.

Only part of the job, she'd say.

Which was how she viewed being married to him? Leaning against the post on the porch, he watched a car slowly drive by. She'd rebuffed all attempts to change the status of their marriage. How clear could a woman make it that she wasn't interested?

But it didn't stop the urges that rose whenever she was around. And it wasn't just that. He loved hearing her laughter, seeing the startled awareness in her eyes when she discovered something new. Seeing the innocent delight she took in being with Mollie.

She was good with Mollie, too. Listened to her, and didn't treat her like an inconvenience.

He hadn't planned on getting married again after failing before. But now that they were married, it wasn't proving as difficult as he'd expected.

Of course not, it wasn't a real marriage. Shelby looked on it as a job. A temporary situation until he found her father and Margot had had her baby. Then she'd take off.

Patrick wasn't sure what he wanted, but it looked more and more as if he didn't want Shelby to leave.

"No work tonight?" Shelby asked as she pushed open the screen door and joined him on the porch.

"No. With the next billing cycle, I think we'll be all caught up. Thanks for your help."

"I enjoyed it. If you need some extra assistance anytime, let me know."

She came to stand near him. Too near. He could smell the sweet scent she wore. Light and fragrant, he'd forever associate it with Shelby.

"It's so hot tonight," she said, sitting on the top step.

Patrick sat beside her, forgetting every resolution to keep his distance. He'd take what he could get.

"The house is cool," he said, still watching the water spray. The sun had set. Darkness cloaked the neighborhood. Lights in the windows of the neighbors' houses shone a warm yellow in the night.

"I know, but I like sitting out. We didn't use the air conditioner a lot when I was younger. So my sisters and I used to walk along the river for whatever breeze was blowing. The spray from the sprinklers would feel good," she said wistfully.

"So go play in it."

Shelby looked at him with those wide eyes of hers. Patrick felt like he'd been hit with a truck. How long did she think he could resist?

"I'd get soaked. The spray is too high to just go wading."

"So, that dress is washable. It'd cool you off."

Patrick could almost see her thought process as she eyed the sprinklers. The temptation was great, he could tell. He wished she felt as tempted by him.

"That would look great to the neighbors, right? Me

cavorting like a four-year-old in the sprinklers," she said slowly.

He smiled. "They can't see anything. It's dark, and the tree casts shadows from the moonlight. Not that I think the neighbors would be outside now anyway. They're all tucked up in their cool homes, windows closed, TV on."

Patrick watched as Shelby scooted off her sandals. She rose and glanced at him.

"Don't you want to cool off?"

He hadn't expected her to invite him. "Sure, I'll take off my shoes. You go on."

He kicked off the running shoes and stood, pulling the shirt off his back. The sultry heat of New Orleans in the summer often had him wishing he could wear less. Tossing the shirt on the steps beside their shoes, he watched as she dallied at the outer fringes of the spray. She almost danced in the water.

Patrick took a deep breath and let out a rebel yell, running into the spray, he swooped Shelby up and swung her around and around in the cascading water.

The shock of cold water made her gasp and she let out a yell.

"Patrick! Have you lost your mind? This water is freezing! Put me down!"

"When you're cooled off. It's great!" He set her on her feet, but kept an arm around her shoulder. The fine spray of the sprinklers soaked them both. Shelby's dress molded her figure. Now he wished he'd put on the porch light. He wanted to see her.

"I'm cool," she laughed, holding her hand out to try to keep the spray from soaking her face. Her hair dripped, hung in wet strands. Suddenly she raised her hands above her head and danced again on the grass, the spray covering them both.

Desire hit suddenly and hard. Patrick caught the laughter as he reached out and pulled her closer, his mouth covering hers. He kissed her, savoring every speck of reaction she gave, pulling her cooled body against his bare chest, ignoring the water that cascaded over them. It no longer felt cool, now it was cold against his heated skin.

When he raised his head, Shelby didn't move. But he could see her wide eyes gazing up into his.

"I want you, Shelby," he said. What an ineffective statement. He yearned for her, craved her. Needed to know everything about her, from where she liked to be touched to how she slept at night. Her taste inflamed him, her scent nearly drove him to his knees. He'd never experienced this with another woman. Why Shelby?

And what was she going to do now?

Shelby shivered in the spray. Patrick surprised her first by pulling her into the middle of the sprinklers, then by his kiss.

Now his statement hung between them. He had not changed his mind! Her heart pounded so hard she could hear the roaring of her blood in her ears. The water no longer did the job of cooling her down.

She was at a crossroads, and unsure what to do next. Hadn't she realized days ago that she was falling in love with this man? Tonight she'd known for certain. And with that love came a curiosity about everything about him. From what his favorite meal was, to what would it be like to make love with him.

She knew he didn't love her, but was wanting enough?

"Shelby?" His lips touched hers again, trailed slow kisses across her cheek and nibbled gently against her earlobe. Her knees felt as strong as gelatine. Her hands twisted themselves behind his neck and she pressed against him. He'd discarded his shirt!

Without conscious thought, her fingers began tracing patterns against his hot skin, feeling the strength of his muscles, the patch of smooth skin on his neck just below his hair. Daringly, she let one hand skim across his bare shoulder and down his muscular chest.

"Say yes, Shelby." He kissed her again and she knew she had to say yes, to give in to his demands, and her own desires.

"Yes, Patrick," she whispered.

He heard her. Sweeping her up into his arms, he headed for the porch.

"I'd love to make love to you beneath the stars, but I want our first time to be special, not complicated by leaves and twigs," he said, mounting the shallow steps that led to the porch.

The first time? Her heart raced.

The cold air in the house sent an instant chill through her, and she snuggled closer. "Guess that sprinkler cooled me down," she murmured, daring to kiss his jaw, let her lips move across his shoulder. His skin was hot, the scent that filled her was Patrick's special one, a mix of soap and cool water and man.

Shelby had never felt so excited in her life! This was the stuff of dreams. How could she inspire such passion? She didn't know, but hoped nothing interfered.

Patrick carried her into his room and nudged the

door shut with his shoulder. Standing her beside the bed, he kissed her again. Grateful her hands were still locked around his neck, she was able to stand. The coolness of the air chilled her where she'd been pressed against Patrick and she shivered.

"You need to get out of those wet clothes," he said softly, already beginning to unfasten the buttons that kept the dress closed.

"I guess you seem to have a head start on me," she said, lightly running her fingertips over the muscles of his chest.

"Oh, honey, if you want to drive me insane, do that one more time," he said, batting her hands away and peeling the dress from her shoulders.

There was scarcely any light coming in through the windows and Shelby felt cocooned in the cool darkness of Patrick's room. She had only peeked in a couple of times to see the room, yet she felt as if it were as familiar as her own.

Standing in just her lacy bra and matching panties, she was suddenly glad for the darkness. She hadn't a clue what to do next. But instinctively, she sought to get closer to Patrick.

"Let me shuck these jeans," he said. The rasp of the zipper sounded above her breath. She heard another sound.

"What's that?" Feeling disoriented, she looked around. Was there someone in the room with them?

"The baby monitor. I use it to keep track of Mollie during the night. If she wakes up and calls, I can hear her in here."

"Is it a two-way setup?" she asked.

"No, she can't hear us. Anyway, she's sound asleep."

She heard the jeans land on the floor and heat enveloped her from head to toe. "Patrick, I'm not sure about this," she began to say. But he cut her off by another kiss.

Before she knew it he'd picked her up again and placed her on the bed. Following her down, his mouth soon had her forgetting everything but the glorious sensations that swept through her.

His hands moved gently against her skin, inflaming her as he sought to learn every inch. His kisses grew deeper, hotter. Shelby thought she would burn up with the heat that invaded each cell. The hunger grew with every passing moment until she thought she would go crazy.

Uncertainty fled. She loved Patrick and wanted to experience that love to the fullest, and in every way possible. Giving in to the instincts that seemed to guide her, she moved her hands over his taut body, finding and giving pleasure as he did with her.

When the final moment arrived, she clutched him tightly and exploded in ecstasy and marvel, holding him closely and cherishing every splendid second. She loved him and had given all she had to show him.

Feeling replete, exhilarated and a bit smug, she turned in his arms some time later.

"Patrick?"

But only silence, and the steady breathing of her husband, was her reply.

"I love you," she whispered, unable to contain the words. "I love you and Mollie."

Would tonight make a change in their marriage?

Would they forget the early terms and set new ones? Shelby hoped so. Believed so.

Slowly she drifted off to sleep, a special glow easing her way.

Shelby woke slowly, moving restlessly. Opening her eyes, she stared at the pillow next to hers. An indentation showed where Patrick had slept, but he had already gone.

Slowly she sat up, no longer feeling like she belonged. Instead she felt out of place. Rising, she picked up her dress—still damp. Wrinkling her nose, she held it in one hand. No way was she going to put it on. She pulled the sheet from the bed and wrapped it around her for the short trip to her own bedroom.

The house was silent. On the way to her room, she peeked into Mollie's. The little girl lay on her stomach, still fast asleep.

Maybe it wasn't as late as she thought it was, Shelby mused as she hurried into her room. The clock said seven fifteen. Why had Patrick left so early? Did he have an early appointment?

Gathering her things, she headed for the bathroom. The warm shower felt good. Dressed a short time later, she again checked on Mollie, then went to the kitchen. She'd make pancakes for the little girl and see how she felt about going to the day care today. If she wasn't up to it, Shelby could skip work, as well.

But Mollie seemed raring to go a few minutes later when she whirled into the kitchen.

"Hi, Shelby. Did you see my stitches. I gots two!"

"Have, honey. You *have* two. And yes, I saw the doctor put them in." And hoped never to go through something like that again. Shelby truly thought it hurt her more than Mollie. The child had a local anesthetic, after all.

"Where's Daddy?"

"Gone to work, I guess."

She found the note leaning against the milk carton. Her heart skipped a beat and Shelby reached for it. He hadn't left without a word, just put the note where she was sure not to miss it.

Lunch around noon?

"Short and to the point," she murmured. What had she expected, protestations of undying love? Just because—

"I'm hungry," Mollie said.

Shelby slipped the note into her pocket and began to fix breakfast. But she couldn't slip away from the tingling sensation of anticipation that curled within. The warm glow that seemed to fill her. Patrick wanted to see her again at lunch! He didn't even want to wait until after work. That had to mean something, right?

It was ten minutes after twelve by the time Shelby entered the investigative offices. She remembered the first time she'd come, how he'd been so impatient to leave to get Mollie. So much had changed since then. Yet it had only been a few weeks.

"Hi, Mrs. O'Shaunnessy," the receptionist said with a warm welcome on her face.

"Hi." Darn, she couldn't remember the woman's name. "I've come to have lunch with Patrick. Is he here?"

"He will be back soon, had to go out on a case a

couple of hours ago. Would you like to wait in his office?''

"Okay." Shelby followed the young woman into Patrick's private office, and gazed around. She'd been in it a couple of times, but just for fleeting visits. Glancing at the different stacks of folders on the desk and credenza, she wondered if he were truly all caught up on the accounts.

Idly moving around, she glanced at two of the stacks. A name caught her eye from a label on a folder midway down the smaller pile. *Sam Williams.*

"Are these accounts awaiting billing?" she asked, looking closer.

"Naw, those are the inactive accounts," the receptionist replied.

"Inactive?" Shelby repeated, puzzled. Wasn't that folder for her father?

"Yes, cases that we're no longer working on for one reason or another."

CHAPTER TEN

SHELBY couldn't move. She glanced at the receptionist, but the woman was already walking back to her desk. When she was out of sight, Shelby shifted the top folders and picked up the one labeled Sam Williams. She crossed to Patrick's desk and sat in his chair, opening the folder.

There were notes and photocopies of faxes. Scanning the loose paper quickly, she flipped to the report sheet stapled to the back of the folder. She knew how he set up the folders, hadn't she worked on enough of them?

From the reports, it looked as if Patrick had located several men who matched some or all of the sketchy information she'd provided. But he had said nothing to her about it. And the final note on the file was over a week old.

What was the folder doing in the inactive stack? A mistake?

A cold feeling settled on Shelby. Or had Patrick deliberately decided to hold off in locating her father to make sure she stuck around to take care of Mollie?

Once the thought popped into her mind, she couldn't shake it.

Last night—had that also been about keeping her around? Watching a four-year-old was difficult when a man had to earn a living and had no one to back him up when work overlapped into Mollie's child care limits. She could understand a man being desperate to keep whatever child care he could.

Feeling sick, Shelby took a deep breath unable to believe he'd stopped work on the search. There had to be some sort of explanation. She thought she could trust him, had depended upon him to do his best to locate her father. Now she questioned that trust. Questioned what her eyes told her had to be true. She had lied to her sisters and friends, pretending to be married, pretending to be in love—all because she had trusted him.

Only, it hadn't all been pretense. Not for her. Just for him.

Shelby didn't know how long she sat there, her mind spinning with different scenarios. None satisfied her. She had the proof in black and white in front of her.

"Hi Shelby, sorry I'm late. I thought I'd be finished before—" Patrick breezed into the office. When he caught sight of her, he stopped abruptly.

Shelby looked up. His face said it all. He dropped his gaze to the opened folder, glanced at the stack of inactive files, then raised his gaze to hers, guilt written all over him.

Slowly he closed the door behind him, shutting the two of them in his office.

"I can explain," he said.

"I can't wait to hear. This is the folder for my father, right?" she asked, closing it and resting her hands on it.

"Yes."

"I found it in the inactive pile."

"Temporarily," he said, stepping closer. He never took his gaze from her.

"So the search was suspended."

"Temporarily," he said again.

"Why?"

Patrick rubbed the back of his neck, glancing around the cluttered office as if searching for inspiration.

Shelby stood, feeling at a disadvantage sitting. Her heart pounded as she waited for Patrick to explain away what she suspected. To have him tell her the folder was in the wrong pile. But so far he hadn't.

"It isn't going to take much longer to narrow the field to the right man," he began. "I guess you read the file?"

She nodded.

"A quick trip to each location, ask a few pointed questions, and we'll be able to verify his identity in no time."

"Then why hasn't it been done already?" she said, keeping her voice even. She refused to let him know how much the discovery hurt her. She felt lied to and betrayed. After all she'd done, she deserved more than this.

"Why did you stop the investigation over a week ago?"

He met her eyes again. "Initially because I needed you to stay with Mollie."

"That was our bargain. I fulfilled my part." Tears threatened. She'd done everything just as they had agreed. Why hadn't he?

"Was keeping a temporary mother so important you'd deliberately delay the search to make sure I didn't leave? I said I'd stay until Margot had her baby and Mollie was settled at school."

He nodded, drew in a deep breath. "You said that,

but I wasn't sure once you had what you wanted you would stay.''

"And rather than give me the chance to decide that, you made sure things went exactly as you wanted by halting the investigation. I thought better of you, Patrick." She picked up the folder and skirted the desk, heading for the door.

"Wait, Shelby, there's more."

"After last night, I guess there is more. How low can a man get?"

Almost running from the office, she didn't even hesitate a second when Patrick called after her.

The elevator was on the floor, its doors about to shut. Squeezing in at the last second, Shelby pushed the down button. She could hear Patrick's voice through the doors just before the car began its descent.

When she reached the sidewalk, she started walking. Her thoughts tumbled. She couldn't focus on anything and yet she needed to think. Try to understand what was going on. And decide what she would do about it. Obviously last night had not been the glorious revelation to Patrick that she'd experienced. In light of what she learned today, it had to have been a ploy to keep her tied to him. At least until he had Mollie situated.

It was stupid to think otherwise. He'd always been honest—he wanted her for an affair. He'd never said anything about love.

Tears threatened again.

"You didn't have to go that far," she said aloud. Two people looked at her oddly as they passed.

She had thought something was building between her and Patrick, certain that the strong feelings she experienced couldn't have been one-sided. Yet she had obviously seen only what she wanted to see. He didn't even care enough for her to complete the search for her father. Or treat her with the respect she deserved.

Anger burned at his callous disregard toward her. She would not have left him in the lurch. She was not Sylvia. She was not anyone except herself, Shelby Beaufort. O'Shaunnessy.

The afternoon sun beat relentlessly on her as she walked aimlessly. When she realized how hot she was, she took stock. Instinct, she thought, when she recognized where she was. Only a few blocks from Georgia's place. Quickly she headed for her sister's apartment, trying to remember if this was one of her days off. She needed family now. The time for pretending she'd found happiness with Patrick was over.

She didn't know what they'd tell Margot, but for now, she needed someone to talk to, to confide in. Someone who wouldn't betray her for his own selfish interests. Who wouldn't lead her on and then let her discover it was all for his own purpose with no consideration for her own sensibilities.

How could she have fallen in love with a man who used people? How could she still wish he could have explained away the folder. If he'd just said it was misplaced, she probably would have believed him.

Georgia opened the door when Shelby rang the bell. Thank goodness for rotating shifts.

"Hi Shelby, you just caught me." Taking a closer look, she reached out to gently grasp Shelby's arm and draw her into the cool apartment. "You look awful. What's wrong?"

At her kind tone, Shelby burst into tears.

"Gee, I guess this isn't a friendly little visit in the

middle of a work day,'' Georgia said hugging her sister. "Come and sit down. Tell Georgia all about it.''

Grabbing a handful of tissues in passing, Georgia led her to the sofa and urged her to sit. Stuffing the tissues into one hand, she took the folder and dropped it onto the coffee table.

"Sorry, I don't usually lose control like this,'' Shelby said as she tried to dry her eyes. "It must be the heat.''

"Uh-huh,'' Georgia agreed.

"Or the humidity.''

"Uh-huh.''

"It's Patrick,'' Shelby said, giving up all thought of further pretense.

"Figures.''

"What?'' She looked up, drying the last of the tears. He was not worth crying over!

"Well, you're usually composed and handle things fine. To be in such a state, I figured it had to be your husband. What happened, you two have a fight?''

"No. But I found out he's not the man I thought he was.''

"Who is he, then?'' Georgia asked, surprised.

"He's a lying, deceitful, selfish, self-serving...*man*. He does nice things, but not to be nice, just to lure me in, make me feel comfortable. To give me hope. Then he stops for no reason except he thinks I'm like his first wife. Which I'm not, but would he let me prove it, oh, no, he made all the decisions and hid everything from me until I found out. Then he didn't lie, just kept looking at me like he wanted to make something up, but of course he can't by now, could he?''

Georgia blinked, and sat down on a chair. "I'm not following this, Shelby," she said slowly.

"The proof is in the folder. The one from the *in-active* pile." Shelby picked up the folder and tossed it to her sister. "I can't believe I let myself believe him. Pretended it might all come right one day. That a man like that could really fall for a woman like me."

"Huh? Now what are you talking about?" Georgia asked as she skimmed through the various sheets in the folder. "Has Patrick located our father?" she asked excitedly.

Shelby surged to her feet and began to pace. "Is that all you can say? My heart is broken and you just ask if he's located our father?"

Georgia's head snapped up at that and she stared at Shelby. "Why is your heart broken?"

"I just explained!"

"No, you didn't. Sit down and tell me, and go slow. I haven't understood a word you've said since you arrived."

Shelby tossed the spent tissues into a wastebasket and calmly sat on the sofa. Explaining to Georgia proved harder than she'd expected. But she covered the entire situation, from the earlier attempts to hire a private investigator until she found the folder at noon. Except for last night. That was personal.

"Wow, Shelby. I would never have expected it of you. Good going!"

"What?"

"That was brilliant, getting him to search for our father. And the coverup was super. I never suspected, and I know Margot didn't. So what's the problem?"

"He stopped looking for our father."

''Temporarily, he said. Just tell him you'll stay until Mollie's set and he'll resume where he left off.''

''He should have known I'd stay.'' Especially after last night.

Georgia looked at her a moment. ''Uh-oh, I just had a thought. Mollie won't stay your stepdaughter when you two separate. Darn, I really like that little girl.''

''Me, too,'' Shelby said, wondering if the tears would overtake her again.

''I think Patrick likes you,'' Georgia said gently.

Shelby shrugged, suddenly listless. She couldn't believe she'd gone from feeling on top of the world this morning to feeling used and discarded this afternoon.

The phone rang.

Georgia picked it up and spoke briefly. Shelby didn't pay attention. She was trying to figure out what to do next. Maybe she could room with Georgia until the sublet was up on her apartment. She'd have to come up with some story for Margot, but she could figure that out later.

''Okay, I'll see you in a few minutes.''

Shelby looked at her as Georgia hung up.

''Who was that?''

''Patrick. He's coming here to see you.''

''No!'' She jumped up. ''I don't want to see him! I'm getting out of here.''

''Wait a minute, Shelby. Give the guy a break. Hear him out. You owe him that much.''

''I don't.''

''What can it hurt?''

Shelby sighed. She couldn't hurt any more than she already did. And she did have to talk to him to arrange to get her things from his home.

What about Mollie? She couldn't just leave without saying goodbye. In fact, Shelby thought, maybe she shouldn't leave at all. At least not until school started. That would show Patrick that his distrust had been misplaced. That she could be counted on to uphold her end of the bargain no matter what!

"Go wash your face, I'll let him in if he gets here before you're finished," Georgia said.

Feeling refreshed and ready to face the world some time later, Shelby walked into the living room, and stopped when she saw Patrick.

"Georgia went for a walk," he said, rising when she entered.

"It's hot out."

"She won't melt. I couldn't catch the elevator."

"How did you know I'd be here?"

He gave a half smile. "I'm a great P.I., remember? Isn't that why you came to me in the first place?"

Shelby could scarcely remember why she'd gone to Patrick's office that first day. She only wished now that she hadn't.

No, that wasn't strictly true. She just wished she hadn't fallen in love with him.

"Sit down, Patrick. Your towering over me makes me nervous."

"Good, then maybe I won't be the only one nervous here."

Startled, Shelby's gaze clashed with his. "You've never been nervous a day in your life." He'd been so calm when dealing with Mollie and her injury, with playing the role of devoted bridegroom, when handling Rand's inquisition.

"Try scared silly," he said stepping closer.

"About what?"

"That I blew things beyond repair."

She shrugged, watching him warily.

Slowly, as if not to frighten a scared puppy, he reached out his hand and cupped the back of her head.

Shelby stiffened. "Don't."

"Shelby, last night was special. But it wasn't the only special part of our relationship. Just being with you is special."

She closed her eyes. Maybe if she didn't have to look at him she could think straight.

"You don't need to sweet-talk me any more, Patrick. I've said I'll stay until after Margot has her baby, and by then Mollie will be settled into her after-school care."

"Good. Then there's just us to discuss."

"There is no us." She opened her eyes and glared up into his. "I can't believe you stopped the investigation."

"I wanted you to stay," he said simply. "I was afraid that if I fulfilled my end of the bargain, you'd take off. Would it have hurt to stall a little longer? You said you just wanted to know about your dad, where he was, what he was doing. A few months one way or another wouldn't matter, would they?"

"I trusted you. I depended on you to uphold your end of the bargain."

"And I will. We didn't discuss time frames. If I deliver the goods by November, I'll have done my part, right?"

His other arm came around her shoulders, drawing her closer and closer until Shelby put her palms up against his chest to keep some space. Only the minute she touched the warmth of his shirt, she longed to cling, not repel.

Which reminded her of last night.

Which instigated the pain she'd felt earlier.

"You didn't have to resort to making love to keep me around," she muttered, her gaze dropping to the column of his throat. The pulse point beat in time to his heart. She had the oddest notion to kiss him and feel that pulse against her lips.

Patrick made a sound that was half laugh, half groan. "Resort to? Shelby, I've wanted you for weeks. Last night was just a man at the end of his tether. It had nothing to do with anything else but how we feel about each other and you know it."

"I don't know anything of the sort. How do you feel about me?" she asked, her own heart starting to pound.

"How do you feel about me?" he countered.

Slowly she let her gaze meet his. Almost holding her breath she wondered if—

"You're the hot-shot P.I., you tell me."

"Babe, you've got me so mixed up I'm lucky I can put my shoes on in the mornings. I can't begin to guess how you feel about me, because I'm so caught up with feelings and emotions that I never expected to experience. I love you, Shelby O'Shaunnessy. I fought against it, denied it as long as I could. Then I didn't want to frighten you off. That had not been part of our agreement, but it didn't matter. I wanted you last night. I still want you. So now you know."

Shelby stared at him in shock for several minutes. Then she slipped her hands up and around his neck.

"You really love me? The man who never planned

to marry again? The man who swore off women for good, except as a baby-sitter for his daughter?''

Resting his forehead against hers, he nodded.

"I can tell you are going to be the kind of wife who says I told you so."

She laughed, her heart soaring. "Patrick, I love you too!"

He almost crushed her in his embrace, his mouth finding hers in a searing kiss.

"Truly?" he asked a few minutes later, searching her eyes for the sincerity she knew he'd find.

"Yes, truly. But I didn't want you to know. I remember all the times you said you didn't want to marry."

"Before I met you, honey. Before I knew you. Stay married to me, Shelby. Let's make a lifetime together."

"Oh, Patrick, yes!" Shelby tightened her grip and kissed him, trying to show him with a single kiss all the love she had for the man of her dreams. He wouldn't always be easy to live with, but she wouldn't have any other.

She pulled back and smiled brightly. "Let's go get Mollie and tell her."

He nodded, releasing her slowly. "Not that she'll get the distinction. She didn't know this was a temporary arrangement."

"No, but I'd like to see her, just the same." She looked at him uncertainly, wistfully. "Do you think maybe down the road we could have her call me Mommy?"

"I expect she'll be delighted to start before the next baby comes."

"Next baby?"

"You didn't want Margot to be the only one having a baby, did you? Mollie can be the big cousin, but wouldn't you like another, one of your very own?"

"Mollie will be my very own, the child of my heart. I love her, Patrick. But yes, I wouldn't mind a whole houseful of kids. And in my house they'll get to run and yell and get dirty and have a dog and everything."

"Slide down bannisters and learn manners at an early age."

"That, too," she said, reaching out to touch the future. Her future was Patrick.

EPILOGUE

"I WANT to see, I want to see," Mollie yelled, jumping up and down.

"You'll get to see it, let Shelby open it first," Patrick said as he handed Shelby the fancy wrapped box.

"What it is?" Shelby asked, reaching up to give her husband a quick kiss. She and Mollie had been home just a few minutes when he walked in.

"Just a little *lagniappe*. See if you like it."

Shelby smiled and walked into the living room. The anticipation built as she delayed. Sitting on the sofa, she gave Patrick a quick glance. A little gift. Her first from Patrick, how could she not love it.

She slipped her finger beneath the edge of the wrapping paper.

In only a moment she withdrew the framed photograph. It was of the two of them on their wedding day. Tears of delight threatened as she traced the line of Patrick's jaw. They looked radiant, just like any couple marrying should look on their special day.

"Wherever did you get this?"

"Your friend Bethany took a whole roll, don't you remember. She asked me if I wanted to have some made up large. I liked that one best."

"And you have the others?"

"All of them. Do you like it?"

"I love it!"

"If you like, I thought we could put it up somewhere," he said diffidently.

"I love it. Almost as much as I love you," she said softly as he sat beside her. Mollie crowded on the other side.

"I want to see, Mommy. I want to see," Mollie said, pulling on Shelby's arm.

Still not used to the name, Shelby felt a warmth in her heart. The same warmth she felt every time she met her husband's eyes. Life was wonderful. Shelby showed her daughter the picture, remembering that day. How things had changed. She was loved, and loved. She was no longer on the outside looking in.

"Oh, Patrick, Georgia called yesterday. She still has the folder on our father and said to tell you she'll bring it in to the office tomorrow. I meant to tell you earlier, but I forgot."

Two small palms bracketed Shelby's cheeks as Mollie stood beside her and turned her face. "For*have*, Mommy, don't say got."

Patrick burst out laughing at Shelby's stunned expression.

"Explain that one away," Patrick dared.

Instead she gathered the little girl in her arms and turned to Patrick, all the love in her shining from her eyes. "I'll just count my blessings instead."

At those words, he leaned over to kiss her and Shelby knew she didn't need to find her father to complete her life. It was complete with Patrick.

Margot, *Shelby* and *Georgia*
are getting married. But first they have
a mystery to solve....

Join these three sisters on the way to the
altar in an exciting new trilogy from

BARBARA McMAHON

in Harlequin Romance

MARRYING MARGOT July 2000

A MOTHER FOR MOLLIE August 2000

GEORGIA'S GROOM September 2000

**Three sisters uncover secrets—
that lead to marriage with
the men of their dreams!**

Visit us at www.eHarlequin.com   HRBEAU

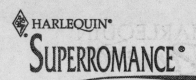

HARLEQUIN®
SUPERROMANCE®

You are now entering

WELCOME TO
RIVERBEND
POPULATION
8793

Riverbend…the kind of place where everyone knows
your name—and your business. Riverbend…home of
the River Rats—a group of small-town sons and
daughters who've been friends since high school.

The Rats are all grown up now. Living their lives and
learning that some days are good and some days
aren't—and that you can get through anything
as long as you have your friends.

Starting in July 2000, Harlequin Superromance brings
you Riverbend—six books about the River Rats and
the Midwest town they live in.

BIRTHRIGHT by Judith Arnold (July 2000)
THAT SUMMER THING by Pamela Bauer (August 2000)
HOMECOMING by Laura Abbot (September 2000)
LAST-MINUTE MARRIAGE by Marisa Carroll (October 2000)
A CHRISTMAS LEGACY by Kathryn Shay (November 2000)

Available wherever Harlequin books are sold.

HARLEQUIN®
Makes any time special ™

Visit us at www.eHarlequin.com   HSRIVER

*It's hard to resist the lure of the
Australian Outback!*

*One of Harlequin Romance's
best-loved Australian authors*

Margaret Way

brings you

Stories in this series are:

A WIFE AT KIMBARA (#3595)
March 2000

THE BRIDESMAID'S WEDDING (#3607)
June 2000

THE ENGLISH BRIDE (#3619)
September 2000

*Available in March, June and September
wherever Harlequin Books are sold.*

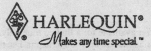

HARLEQUIN®
Makes any time special.™

Visit us at www.eHarlequin.com   HRLOTO

HARLEQUIN

Duets™

Pick up a Harlequin Duets™
from August–October 2000
and receive $1.00 off the
original cover price. *

Experience the "lighter side of love"
in a Harlequin Duets™*.*
This unbeatable value just became
irresistible with our special introductory
price of $4.99 U.S./$5.99 CAN. for
2 Brand-New, Full-Length
Romantic Comedies.

Offer available for a limited time only.
Offer applicable only to Harlequin Duets™.
*Original cover price is $5.99 U.S./$6.99 CAN.

Visit us at www.eHarlequin.com   HDMKD

HARLEQUIN®
SUPERROMANCE®

Here's what small-town dreams are made of!

BORN IN A SMALL TOWN

is a special 3-in-1 collection featuring

New York Times bestselling author
Debbie Macomber's brand-new Midnight Sons
title, *Midnight Sons and Daughters*

Judith Bowen's latest Men of Glory title—
The Glory Girl

Janice Kay Johnson's story, returning to
Elk Springs, Oregon—*Promise Me Picket Fences*

Join the search for romance in three small towns
in September 2000.

Available at your favorite retail outlet.

HARLEQUIN®
Makes any time special ™

Visit us at www.eHarlequin.com   HSRBORN

**Don't miss
an exciting opportunity
to save on the purchase of
Harlequin and Silhouette books!**

Buy any two Harlequin or
Silhouette books and save
$10.00 off future Harlequin
and Silhouette purchases

OR

buy any three
Harlequin or Silhouette books
and save **$20.00 off** future
Harlequin and Silhouette purchases.

**Watch for details
coming in October 2000!**

PHQ400

HARLEQUIN®
Makes any time special ™

Silhouette
Where love comes alive ™

Romance is just one click away!

online book serials

- *Exclusive* to our web site, get caught up in both the daily and weekly online installments of new romance stories.
- Try the Writing Round Robin. Contribute a chapter to a story created by our members. Plus, winners will get prizes.

romantic travel

- Want to know where the best place to kiss in New York City is, or which restaurant in Los Angeles is the most romantic? Check out our Romantic Hot Spots for the scoop.
- Share your travel tips and stories with us on the romantic travel message boards.

romantic reading library

- Relax as you read our collection of Romantic Poetry.
- Take a peek at the Top 10 Most Romantic Lines!

Visit us online at

www.eHarlequin.com
on Women.com Networks

HEUT1

Daddy's little girl... **THAT'S MY BABY!** by

Vicki Lewis Thompson

Nat Grady is finally home—older and wiser. When the woman he'd loved had hinted at commitment, Nat had run far and fast. But now he knows he can't live without her. But Jessica's nowhere to be found.

Jessica Franklin is living a nightmare. She'd thought things were rough when the man she loved ran out on her, leaving her to give birth to their child alone. But when she realizes she has a stalker on her trail, she has to run—and the only man who can help her is Nat Grady.

THAT'S MY BABY!

On sale September 2000 at your favorite retail outlet.

HARLEQUIN®
Makes any time special ™

Visit us at www.eHarlequin.com   PHTMB